She had never known a kiss like this

Finally his lips lifted, and Dena made a small, bereft sound. Then she tilted her head and smiled. The touch of his warm cheek, abrasive with a day's beard, could be addicting, she decided. With a sigh, she tugged at the back of his neck and brought his lips back to hers.

Later, still struggling for breath, he stepped back, keeping his hands on her shoulders. "The last thing in the world I want to do is walk away from you tonight. You know that, don't you?"

Speechless, she nodded.

"So I'm going to get out of here while I still can," he continued grimly. "Unless you want me to stay?"

Dear Reader,

Although our culture is always changing, the desire to love and be loved is a constant in every woman's heart. Silhouette Romances reflect that desire, sweeping you away with books that will make you laugh and cry, poignant stories that will move you time and time again.

This year we're featuring Romances with a playful twist. Remember those fun-loving heroines who always manage to get themselves into tricky predicaments? You'll enjoy reading about their escapades in Silhouette Romances by Brittany Young, Debbie Macomber, Annette Broadrick and Rita Rainville.

We're also publishing Romances by many of your all-time favorites such as Ginna Gray, Dixie Browning, Laurie Paige and Joan Hohl. Your overwhelming reaction to these authors has served as a touchstone for us, and we're pleased to bring you more books with Silhouette's distinctive medley of charm, wit and—above all—*romance*. I hope you enjoy this book, and the many stories to come.

Sincerely,

Rosalind Noonan
Senior Editor
SILHOUETTE BOOKS

RITA RAINVILLE
Written on the Wind

Silhouette Romance

Published by Silhouette Books New York

America's Publisher of Contemporary Romance

To the Lakewood-Ojai card club gang,
living proof that women form strong bonds of
love and support.

SILHOUETTE BOOKS
300 E. 42nd St., New York, N.Y. 10017

RITA RAINVILLE

grew up reading truckloads of romances and replotting the endings of sad movies. She has always wanted to write the kind of romances she likes to read. She finds people endlessly interesting and that is reflected in her writing. She is happily married and lives in California with her family.

Chapter One

"I'm one of Charlie's secret weapons."

Dena Trevor watched the grim-faced man sitting across from her absorb the words. "Only he and John know that I'm on retainer."

Responding to the taut silence, she continued, "I'm a graphoanalyst." At his blank look, she said, "You know, a handwriting expert." The succinct explanation offered, Dena sat back waiting for the predictable reaction. Other than a raised brow, it didn't come.

Glancing at her watch, Dena stared in disbelief. Had it only been ten minutes ago that she had cracked open the door marked, "John Salcedo, Director of Personnel," wincing when she heard a softly menacing question?

"Where the hell is he?"

John had stood behind his tidy desk like a belea-guered David facing a chestnut-haired Goliath. "He was a security risk."

"You knew that I wanted him on the job today?"

"Yes."

She hadn't met the deep-voiced man before, didn't particularly want to meet him now, she'd decided, but it wasn't fair to let John bear the brunt of his anger. After all, she *had* started the whole thing.

"So you countermanded my direct order?"

"No." Dena took a deep breath, hoped she looked more confident than she felt and stepped in, closing the door behind her. "I did."

The big man pivoted slowly and surveyed her, jolting her with the impact of furious gray eyes. "And just who in God's name are you?"

John filled the silence automatically. "Brand McAllister, meet Dena Trevor."

Brand stepped closer and Dena looked up, higher than she ordinarily had to. He towered a good eight inches above her five-and-a-half feet. His bur-nished hair was short but stylish. Deep slashes in lean cheeks, and peaked brows gave him a danger-ous look. A broad-shouldered, narrow-hipped body that moved with athletic grace only enhanced it.

"I'm the one your Uncle Charlie left behind to tug on the reins if they needed tightening," Dena replied recklessly.

"The hell you are." The hard face—not a bit handsome, she decided, but fascinating if you liked the rakehell type—grew grimmer. "I'm in charge here."

"Of course you are." Her words could have carried more conviction, but they didn't. Her tone could have been more conciliating, but after one look at his assured stance, it wasn't. "But you weren't here to mind the shop in a time of crisis, and that's how I got involved."

If his expression was anything to go by, maybe Charlie's idea hadn't been such a great one after all, Dena thought with another quick glance.

"John—" Brand said abruptly, looking at the slim, dark-haired man "—I'll see you later. Miss Trevor—" he turned back to her with an expressionless face "—we'll finish our discussion in my office."

He ushered her out of the room, a hand on her elbow, propelling her down the wide and airy hall as his long legs made mincemeat of the distance.

"Wait a minute," she said, digging in her heels and pulling him to a stop. "If you're in such a hurry, why don't you trot ahead? Just let your secretary know I'll be trailing in behind you."

"Sorry," he muttered impatiently, tightening his grip on her elbow.

She looked pointedly at his hand, refusing to move. A muscle in his jaw tightened, but he finally released her.

"Thank you," she said in an unruffled voice.

Two minutes later, after telling his slim, middle-aged secretary he was not to be disturbed, they were seated, separated by the width of his desk.

Dena's hands rested quietly in her lap as he surveyed her. She knew what he was seeing. Hadn't she been looking at it in the mirror for almost twenty-seven years? Miss Average U.S.A. Average height and weight, average light-brown hair, average nose and mouth. Gold-flecked eyes with an extravagant frame of dark-brown lashes balanced the scale a bit. But all in all, it wasn't a face or body to provoke wars or induce heavy breathing in her male acquaintances.

Her fingers tightened on the handle of her slim briefcase as the silence stretched out. Why didn't the blasted man say something instead of just sitting there and watching her? Never in her life had she been the object of such a concentrated scrutiny.

She didn't trust the sudden gleam in those cool, gray eyes. It tugged at her memory. She had seen that expression recently, but where? "How's Charlie?" she asked, hoping to divert his silent regard. "I haven't heard from him since he left."

"He bounced back from the heart attack, but the doctor told him to stay away for at least a year unless he wanted a return trip ticket to the hospital."

Dena missed the vigorous silver-haired man who had hired her two years before. Still in his early fifties, he was one of the pioneers of Silicon Valley. Charlie had had a key role in inventing the integrated circuit, the computer chip that is the brains of virtually all modern electronic equipment.

A man of immense wealth, his home company sprawled through the Santa Clara Valley, just south of San Francisco. He had been a late entry into the dog-eat-dog world of personal computers but, typically, was on the verge of still another dramatic breakthrough.

She wished, not for the first time, that Charlie was sitting across from her. It wouldn't have been easy explaining the situation but at least he trusted her. This man, with his quelling gaze and abrupt voice, made it infinitely more difficult.

"Why did you do it?" he finally asked.

She didn't pretend to misunderstand. "Because I'm paid to. Believe me—" she looked at him earnestly, putting aside her personal feelings "—my reaction would have been no different if Charlie had been here."

"Exactly how do you fit in?" Brand asked in a neutral voice. "And where? I thought I had met everyone. At least everyone who had the authority to do something like this," he added dryly.

Good Lord, the man hadn't been told about her! He had reason to be upset. "I just work for Charlie," she replied lightly, wondering how to explain.

"You work for me," he informed her softly. "But doing what?"

If the extended silence was any indication, Dena decided, he hadn't liked her answer. She looked at his thoughtful expression and wondered what was going on behind those silvery eyes.

Brand leaned forward, his unblinking gaze on her face. He was in no hurry, taking in her charcoal suit and red silk blouse. Definitely a professional. But a graphoanalyst? Good God.

His fingers itched to touch the dark-blond hair that was coiled in a silky swirl atop her head. Full brows arched over wide-set eyes. High cheekbones framed a generous mouth and a determined chin. Intelligent, he decided, meeting her level gaze. Confident, too, despite a telltale look of vulnerability around her mouth. And provocative. Provocative as hell and completely unaware of it.

Brand nodded slowly. "Charlie did tell me about you. That is, about having someone on retainer. He never mentioned your name. He also said that you earned your pay, which is high praise for Charlie."

And I'm about to earn it now, she thought grimly.

"My work here is fairly routine and usually confined to personnel matters," she explained slowly, watching his reaction. "John will ask me if an applicant is well-suited for a particular position, or can be trusted with classified information."

She blinked thoughtfully. "Your latest candidate, the engineer you were grilling John about, wasn't routine. I became concerned about the character traits his writing revealed. I advised John to get on the phone and personally check the man's references."

"And?"

"It was like pulling teeth to get his former employers to talk, but John's very good at his job. He found exactly what I thought he would. Your man is brilliant and has all the qualifications you need, but he was let go for selling information. The company couldn't prove it and didn't charge him with anything, but they had no doubt that he was guilty."

Brand muttered a soft, succinct oath.

"That's the good news," Dena said dryly. "Should I go on?"

He nodded grimly.

"John became interested in my work during the two years I've been with the company and has learned quite a bit. He occasionally sends me a sample of writing that catches his eye for one reason or another. In yesterday's mail, I found one that had disturbed him. With good reason," she finished slowly.

Dena was aware of a sudden fixed interest in the gray eyes.

"John said he found the note in the building where the research and development of your new computer is going on. The wording," she said slowly, "is innocuous, just a memo of some sort. But the writer was under great stress, a lot of anger. Combined with certain character traits, it means that you could have a big problem on your hands."

Brand leaned forward, his gaze intent. "What traits?"

"Strong signs of acquisitiveness, resentment and deceit, just to mention a few."

She sat in composed silence for a moment. When no comment was forthcoming, she continued. "I realize that high-tech jobs are usually stressful. The anger could have been caused by any number of things, a co-worker, a momentary feeling of frustration, anything. But the other traits aren't so easily explained."

Her eyes reflected her anxiety. "All of my experience tells me, Mr. McAllister, that in one of your most sensitive areas, you have a walking timebomb!"

Dena watched as Brand leaned back, his face expressionless. He rested his elbows on the arms of his chair, unconsciously steepling his fingers as he gazed at a picture on the wall. Her eyes followed his and she found herself looking at a matted photo of Charlie's first building in Sunnyvale. The motionless man was more interesting, she decided, swiveling back to face him.

She was surprised at his quiet concentration. She had seen his name scrawled boldly on various papers and, despite the fact that she never made an analysis on a signature alone, had reached several conclusions. He thrived on adversity. In fact, when things got dull, he'd go out looking for new challenges. He also had enough leashed energy to keep Charlie's plant running during a power failure. Not a comfortable man to be around, she had concluded.

Her eyes ranged over the massive shoulders covered by a black sport coat. Neither the gray striped shirt nor the splash of a red silk tie could conceal the fact that they covered pure muscle. He looked like he had been carved from a chunk of granite, and his features echoed the same strength and uncompromising quality. There was a hard line to his jaw and his gray eyes were almost colorless with concentration.

Obviously there was much more to be learned about the man. She had been prepared for him to bark out orders and send for the bloodhounds. But this silent, power-packed immobility was getting on her nerves.

Since he was apparently still lost in thought, she continued her survey. Guessing that he must be thirty-four or five, she decided the years had been spent in a tough school. He had the look of a man who knew exactly what he wanted, spared no effort to get it, and willingly paid the price. Then he made sure that he got full value.

That was none of her business, Dena reminded herself bracingly as her gaze dropped to the desktop and drifted idly over several bulky folders. She had done her part, the rest was up to him. Once this meeting was over, she could forget him. She would drive the few miles to her home, kick off her shoes, hang up her suit, put on some comfortable jeans, and get to work on a less troublesome client. She would... Her head tilted sideways as she once again eyed the folders—she would give her eyeteeth to get her hands on the piece of paper facing him.

The thought had barely surfaced, shocking Dena with its intensity, before she again curled her twitching fingers tightly around the handle of her briefcase. Even looking at the writing upside down, she could tell it was his. The temptation to snatch the paper and examine it while he was preoccupied was almost overwhelming. Closing her eyes, she reminded herself that although she was impulsive, she wasn't crazy. People who acted impetuously usually suffered unpleasant consequences, and curiosity almost inevitably killed the cat.

After counting slowly to ten, then adding another ten for good measure, she opened her eyes, jerking in surprise as she found his gray gaze riveted on her face.

His eyes gleamed as they leisurely examined her full pink lips. Dena didn't trust that look. It was too intent, too personal. All told, it was thoroughly male. Just as Brand McAllister himself was, she thought nervously. It was the look of someone bent on satisfying his curiosity and not a bit concerned that he was being obvious. With a shock she identified the other, more elusive expression. It was the same look her three-year-old nephew had on his face when he opened his last birthday gift and found exactly what he'd been hoping for.

"What were you thinking about just now?" The deep voice recalled her errant thoughts.

"That I'd give a lot to look at that paper you've been working on," she confessed, relieved his question hadn't been more personal.

"Are you so interested in what goes on around here?"

"Not a bit," she admitted absently, her eyes glued on the swiftly scrawled words. "It's your writing I want to look at."

Deliberately turning the paper over, he shook his head slowly from side to side. "No way, lady. Anything you learn about me will be firsthand, not from some conclusions you've drawn after looking at a scribbled message."

"You think graphoanalysis is a lot of nonsense, don't you?" she challenged.

His honesty surprised her.

"I don't know anything about it, but Charlie and John seem to think it works. Why don't you tell me about it?" he suggested.

Dena stared suspiciously at the suddenly bland man. "Tell you what?"

"For starters, what made you so sure you were right when you told John to do some snooping about that engineer I wanted him to hire? Is graphoanalysis—my God, what a mouthful—a science?"

"Of course!"

"Recognized in this country as such?"

"Almost."

"So it's not a true science."

The flat statement irritated her. "Yes, it is, but it's also an art," she added honestly.

"How so?" Skepticism was written all over his face.

Knowing that she was dealing with an engineer and had to appeal to his logic, Dena slowly gathered her thoughts. "There's a scientific method of analyzing handwriting, but its interpretation is an art," she said slowly, knowing she couldn't do justice to the subject in just a few minutes. "Each stroke in a letter has its individual meaning, yet it's impossible to base an analysis on separate individual signs. They have to be interpreted as a whole."

He nodded.

"For instance, the way you cross a 't' may reflect one trait in your writing, but only a rank amateur would stop there. That trait could become important or totally insignificant when correlated to all the other signs in your handwriting."

"What if I disguised my writing?"

"You couldn't. At least not for long. You can't fool a pro."

"And you're a pro?"

"I am," she said with calm assertion.

"So what do you plan to do now?" he asked abruptly.

"What do you mean? I've *done* my part. The rest is up to you."

"No way, lady. You don't drop in out of the blue, tell me something I already know, and walk out the door saying you've earned your money."

Her head jerked up in surprise. Gold-flecked eyes met steady gray ones. "You knew?"

His nod was grim. "I found out about that security leak last week. Information on our new computer is getting out."

"Then why haven't *you* done something?"

"What do you suggest?" he asked brusquely. "That I have the entire department arrested?" His gaze still held hers. "What would you do if Charlie were here?"

"Exactly what I've done," she said promptly. "I'd tell him, just as I told you."

"Then what?"

"How do I know? This has never happened before," she admitted. "I assumed that once I told you, my part was over."

"Just like that?" he asked noncommittally.

She nodded in agreement. "Just like that."

His silence informed her that she was dead wrong.

"Look—" she burst out "—this place is bristling with security officers. They're trained for this sort of thing. Go tell them."

"How do you think I found out in the first place?" he asked quietly.

"Oh."

"You did say you were Charlie's secret weapon, didn't you?" he prodded.

"Yes, I did," she admitted, regretting her earlier taunt. "But I don't know what you expect me to do. I'm not a private investigator or a psychic. I don't come equipped with a gun or a crystal ball. The only place I solve mysteries is at my desk."

His voice was smooth with satisfaction. "Exactly, and that's one of the reasons why I want you."

She eyed him dubiously, aware there was a male declaration of intent threaded in his bland voice. Surely he couldn't mean... Of course he didn't.

"Well—" she began politely "—I'll be happy to examine any samples you want to send—"

"No."

"No, what?" she asked with foreboding.

"No, I'm not going to send anything. I want you here."

"I have other clients to take care of," she said reasonably. "Surely you can understand that."

"I think this problem is more urgent than your usual run of personnel forms, don't you?"

"Of course, but—"

"Unless you're afraid you couldn't do it."

"Do what?"

"Properly identify the handwriting. Be able to find the person we're looking for."

"There's no question of that," she said calmly. "Your work applications have a space for a hand-written statement. If I had access to your personnel files, I could compare writings with the sample I have. When I found the one that matched, and did an analysis of it, my testimony would stand up in any court of law."

She watched as he struggled to conceal his skepticism. She didn't know why he even bothered. He was doing a rotten job of it. And why on earth did he want her if he didn't think she could accomplish anything? It didn't make sense.

Anger brought out the gold in her eyes. Whether he believed it or not, she knew how simple it would be to recognize the handwriting of "X." What seemed magical to others was, with the proper training, really quite simple. The time-consuming part would be sifting through the masses of records.

Wouldn't it be nice to prove him wrong? She allowed herself a moment of pure fantasy in which she found "X" in record time, dropped him or her in Brand McAllister's lap and delighted in his look of chagrin. She basked for a moment in the warmth of that extremely satisfying thought. It would be interesting to see if he still remained a skeptic.

Unaware that the man across from her was regarding her expressive face with unblinking concentration, Dena's mouth curved in a pleased smile. "Yes," she repeated, "I could do it."

"Good," Brand said with surprising alacrity. "Where do you live?"

"In Cupertino, near the college. Why?"

"What's your address?"

She rattled it off automatically before asking, "What do you need it for?"

He wrote swiftly, folded the paper and put it in his pocket before he looked up. "So I can pick you up for dinner." He rose smoothly and she almost followed his lead.

"Wait a minute," she said, stubbornly remaining seated. "Who said anything about dinner?"

"I did. Just now. We've got a lot to settle before tomorrow."

"Why? What's happening tomorrow?"

"You start your new job. Here at Mitchell's. Full-time."

Dena closed her eyes and took a deep breath, fully aware that the annoying man towering over her had not taken his eyes off her. He was definitely getting on her nerves, and taking too damn much for granted.

Before Dena could open her mouth, the provoking man was at it again.

"You have a contract, remember?"

Dena opened her eyes and stared stonily up at him. Charlie, with his customary attention to details, had had his lawyers alter their verbal agreement into an airtight contract for the duration of his absence. Not exclusive, he'd assured her. She could continue business as usual with all of her clients, just consider it a mutual insurance policy. She couldn't be fired, but when the work flow demanded it, she would be available. It had sounded reasonable at the time. Now, looking at Charlie's nephew and successor, she wasn't so sure.

"Even though Charlie neglected to mention your name, he did tell me about the contract. It was drawn up so you'd be on call if you were needed."

Brand didn't move, but Dena shifted, feeling a bit claustrophobic.

"You're needed, Dena."

She looked away. What on earth was going on? Without a word Brand McAllister had made it obvious that, as far as he was concerned, she might as well be practicing voodoo. So why was he pushing so hard?

"Charlie said he didn't want me coming to the plant," she said stubbornly, admitting to herself that her resistance wasn't to the work, but to the dark man standing before her. If Charlie had been here, she would have volunteered.

"He also said that the fewer people who knew about me, the more effective I'd be. For heaven's sake, this is the first time I've been to this place since the day he hired me," she ended in obvious irritation.

Brand leaned against the desk and crossed his arms. "Then how did you manage to get so chummy with my uncle?"

Dena's eyes widened at the insinuation but she answered quietly. "Mostly over the telephone, but sometimes he'd drop by my office."

"You'll be in no danger here," he said abruptly, after a thoughtful pause.

She raised startled eyes to his. "That never occurred to me, but now that you've raised the point, if you can't safeguard a secret, how do you plan to protect me?"

"With a cover story. We can always say you're from an agency, hired to help my secretary meet a deadline. Apparently this office calls in temps frequently."

She shook her head thoughtfully. "That's not very efficient. *If* I came, it would be to personnel. That's where all the records are."

"No."

"What do you mean 'no'? Would you expect me to sneak around the building emptying wastepaper baskets and hauling the loot back to this office? Every file, every bit of information I need, including samples of handwriting, is in personnel."

He frowned down at her, a grim set to his lips. "No. I don't want you running around the place causing a lot of speculation. "I've said I'll take care of you and I will. You won't be in any danger if you're in this office where I can keep an eye on you."

"I can just see how much work I'd get done with you popping in and out to see if I'm still in one piece," she muttered.

His voice was as grim as his expression. "Believe me, I wouldn't bother you if Charlie wasn't so convinced that—"

"That what?" she asked when it was obvious that he had no intention of finishing his statement. Waiting, she eyed him sharply.

"Nothing."

The man was as subtle as a tank. Nothing indeed. "Charlie believes in my work," she thought aloud, watching his face. "He wouldn't like it if he found out that some shenanigans were going on around here and you didn't get in touch with me." She watched in fascination as a muscle rippled in his jaw.

"So that's it—" she said slowly. "You only want me here because if Charlie gets wind of this, you can tell him his expert was on the job. You really don't expect me to be of any help, do you?"

Brand's silence was all the affirmation Dena needed.

Dena was shaken by sudden fury. This man's total disregard for her training was insulting. He wasn't even open-minded enough to learn more before he condemned it. What was worse, he expected her to sit at a desk, occupying space, so Charlie would be satisfied that all efforts had been made to plug the leak.

She rose with proud grace. It brought her closer to him than she cared to be, but she refused to back up.

"I'm not going to play your little game." She noted absently that her voice had dropped a notch. It usually did when she was angry. "I have too much work to do to come down here and spin my wheels. Believe it or not, I have clients who actually believe that I offer something of value."

She walked to the door and stopped as her hand touched the knob. Turning, she said, "You know what really ticks me off? I was actually considering it. I was going to find your Mr. X and give him to you as a present." Her icy look dared him to interrupt. "But it'll be a cold day in hell before I lift a finger to help you, Mr. McAllister. And don't worry about that contract. Charlie was only trying to protect me. He'd never hold me to it."

She opened the door and turned back for one parting shot. "Don't change your mind and come to me for help. It's obvious I'm not scientific enough for you. If you really get in a bind...you can try looking up witch doctors in the yellow pages."

The closing door cut off a softly uttered, very nasty word.

Chapter Two

Six hours later, he was leaning on her doorbell.

Ten minutes before, she had eased into the bathtub and elbowed away the bubbles so she could lean back without wetting her hair. Eight minutes later, the chimes informed her that she had a visitor. They had been ringing continuously ever since.

He'll go away, she had assured herself. She didn't doubt for a minute that Brand McAllister was standing outside her door. A salesman would ring once, possibly twice; a neighbor or friend would do the same. She knew only one person who would keep his finger on the bell until she answered.

"I'll murder him," she decided, heaving herself up and starting a minor tidal wave in the tub. "If I can reach his throat, I'll strangle him." Ignoring the water sloshing over the rim, Dena reached for a towel and dried herself with furious energy.

The chimes accompanied muttered maledictions as she stomped into the bedroom and reached for a robe. Grabbing the first one at hand, she thrust her arms into the sleeves and tied it snugly around her waist while heading for the door. Throwing it open, she glared up into smokey gray eyes.

"Exactly what do you want?" Her icy words came slowly through gritted teeth.

"You," he said, fitting his hands around her waist and lifting her as if she weighed nothing at all.

She eyed his neck, wondering if her hands would reach around it. The crisp brown hair showing through the unbuttoned opening of his shirt distracted her momentarily. Her bare feet touched the floor before she could decide, and Brand reached back, closing the door behind him.

"Nice," he said, taking in the mauve velour robe that faithfully clung to her soft, damp curves, "but hardly the thing to wear to dinner."

She stared at him in speechless wonder.

"And your hair's coming down." He reached out a large hand to remove a pin and lightly touched another strand as it fell to her shoulders. "Nice," he repeated. "I like it down like that."

Dena recovered her senses and voice at the same time. Moving out of his reach, she said in a tone that should have felled him on the spot, "If it ever seems important, I'll remember that."

Brand shrugged out of his soft leather jacket and dropped it on the arm of a chair. He stood with his back to her, hands on hips, examining a water-color hanging over the sofa. He had changed into something more casual. He looked different in slacks and a long-sleeved knit shirt. Still massive, still potentially dangerous, but different.

"I don't know about you," he commented, still staring at the painting, "but I'm hungry."

"That's too bad," she said with a remarkable lack of sympathy. "When I left your office—"

"In high dudgeon," he murmured.

"What?" Her voice was as blank as her expression.

"In high dudgeon. I always wondered what that meant. I found out this afternoon."

He sounded satisfied, she thought, as if he had just solved some impossible mathematical equation.

"I'm glad you learned something, but apparently the rest of my message went over your head."

He turned, looking down at her with thoughtful gray eyes. "You said you wouldn't help me. You didn't say a thing about canceling our dinner date."

He's been around computers too long; he's beginning to think like them, was her first reaction. Her second was a tug of fascination. Never in her life had Dena run across such a literal person. Her third reaction was the reappearance of her sense of humor. That, she decided later, was her downfall.

Her voice was solemn. "You're absolutely right. I forgot to tell you that."

An hour later, she was saying with asperity, "That's not the way it works."

She was sitting across from Brand in a small Italian restaurant. Dena had been greeted with a bellow of delight from a brawny man with dark, thick hair. After hugging her, he turned his attention to Brand. Keen brown eyes observed the carved features and the possessive hand Brand deliberately placed on her shoulder. With a wide smile, he led them to a back table. He had not seated anyone near them.

After working her way through a salad and a huge slab of delicious lasagna, Dena was still trying to clear up Brand's misconceptions about her profession.

"I can't tell people what the future holds for them. And I can't answer general questions."

His eyes followed her slim hand as she emphasized the point with a gesture equivalent to a shrug. "Such as?"

Adding cream to her coffee, she said in exasperation, "Just last week, a woman asked me if her boyfriend loved her. I couldn't tell her. Then she asked me if he was married. I couldn't make her understand that marriage doesn't change a person's basic traits, and that's what an analysis is based on."

"What else can't you tell?"

"The age or sex of the writer."

Brand straightened slowly. "You mean that—"

She nodded. "Right. Your Mr. X could just as easily be Ms X, right out of school or near retirement."

Well, something had finally gotten through to him and erased that look of tolerance. It also removed the gleam from his eyes—the one he made no effort to mask. The one that had kept her on edge since he had walked into her living room.

"I don't believe it," he said flatly. "For God's sake, *I* can do that much."

"No you can't." Her contradiction was just as flat. "What you do is recognize certain handwritings, say those of your family or friends. If you receive a letter from Charlie, you know it's from him without even looking at the return address because you *recognize* the writing. Since Charlie is a male, you unconsciously label his writing as masculine. You do the same thing with a letter from a woman. But I could put ten or twenty sample letters in front of you, and you couldn't tell the difference."

She grinned at his look of disbelief. "Trust me. I know what I'm talking about."

"I suppose you do," he said finally. His attempt to balance tact and doubt failed miserably.

Her voice was dry. "Thanks for the vote of confidence."

"What do you expect? So far, all you've told me is what you don't and can't do. Why don't you explain how it works? You might start with the scientific aspect," he suggested, straight faced.

She eyed him with disfavor. "I tried that once," she reminded him, "and all I got for my efforts was a patronizing pat on the head."

His eyes flickered with an expression she couldn't interpret. "All right," she said abruptly. "But so help me, if you so much as lift an eyebrow, I'm walking out of here. And you can ring my doorbell till your finger falls off, but I won't open the door."

He nodded.

Placing her cup carefully in her saucer, she said, "First of all, handwriting should probably be called *mind* writing because your brain impels your hand. It transmits impulses, and the motor nervous system controls every movement of writing. Your writing expresses your personality just as much as your walk and talk does.''

Brand nodded again, understanding why she had rid herself of the cup. She probably couldn't utter a sound if her hands were tied down. ''There've been articles in papers and magazines about it lately—'' he acknowledged ''—but I've been wrapped up in some research and haven't paid much attention to them. Is this a new field?'' He carefully avoided the word 'science.'

She shook her head. ''Hardly. Aristotle was talking about it in the third century B.C. Through the ages various historians and philosophers have studied the subject. One thing they determined is that writing reveals the psychological personality of the writer, not the physiological.''

Her eyes met his. ''That should interest you because it led to the understanding that writing doesn't reveal the age or sex of the writer. Proven scientifically,'' she added dryly, ''through thousands of tests and consistent results.''

She took a sip of coffee, her eyes quizzical over the edge of the cup. ''Any questions?''

''Yes. How did you get involved in graphology?''

Dena retreated to the back of her chair. He had obviously switched his concentration from the graphoanalyst to the woman, and she didn't welcome the change.

''When I was fifteen I went to a county fair. Since there wasn't a fortune-teller around, I had my handwriting analyzed.''

His warm hand engulfed her cool one as it rested on the table. Turning it, he laced her slim fingers through his own and murmured, "I think I'm sorry I asked."

She tried, and failed, to slip her hand from his grasp. "Have I just blown my credibility?"

He shook his head, looking more relaxed than she had yet seen him. What would it take to make the man laugh, she wondered.

"Are you ready to go?"

She nodded, surprised at his abrupt shift of conversation. "It's a good thing you ate your lasagna," she said as he dropped several bills on the table. "Otherwise, Leo would have been back here watching every bite we took. If people don't clean their plates, he's convinced they hate the food."

"Then he shouldn't serve portions the size of a shoe box."

"You're right—" she sighed "—but you'll never convince him."

"Known him long?" The question seemed wrung out of him against his will.

"Most of my life. He's my best friend's older brother. We all went to the same schools here in Santa Clara."

As they approached the door, their host hurried to them. With a final hug for Dena and a murmured message, he let them go.

"What did he say?" Brand asked as they buttoned their jackets against the brisk fall air.

"Hmm? Oh, something about his sister." It was a lie. Leo had whispered, "Careful, *cara*. This one isn't the type you usually bring in here. And he wants you."

His hand in the small of her back urged her gently toward the red Porsche. "Are you going to ask me in for a nightcap?" he asked, opening her door and watching as she buckled her seat belt. He closed it before she could answer.

He walked around the front of the car, slid into his side and started the motor. "Well?"

"If you want more coffee or a glass of wine, you're invited," she said, as he swung out into the traffic.

"That's all you have?"

"That's all I like. Why have stuff around that I don't drink?"

"For someone else?" he suggested.

"It hasn't caused a problem so far."

Without a word, he pulled to a stop in front of a market. "Be right back."

He was. Within minutes he returned carrying a large brown paper sack and dumped it gently in her lap. "Take good care of that."

As he headed east on Stevens Creek Boulevard, Dena examined the contents of the bag. "Good grief, there's enough in here to stock a small store. What are you going to do with it?"

"Leave it at your house—"

"But I told you—"

"So there'll be something to drink when I come by."

"Are you planning on a siege?"

"If necessary."

Dena couldn't think of an adequate reply and settled for silence. It lasted until they reached her town house. She had her key ready and they hurried in, closing out the blustery wind.

"Where do you want this?" Brand jiggled the bag.

"On the kitchen bar for now. I'll figure out where to put it later. Unless you decide to take it—"

"No."

Someday, Dena decided, she was going to have a long talk with him about making requests instead of assumptions. Undoubtedly other things would be added to the list.

"Want anything?" he asked, neatly lining up the bottles.

"No thanks." Opening the refrigerator, she withdrew a bottle of Riesling. "I'll have some of this."

She watched as he poured Scotch in a glass, added water, put the glass down, capped the bottle and wiped the gleaming tile. His movements were automatic rather than fussy. His house was probably depressingly neat, she thought, glancing around her comfortably rumpled place as she led the way into the living room. She didn't know how it happened, but every flat surface was an invitation to clutter. Everywhere she looked, something was where it shouldn't have been.

A notepad and pencils were next to the telephone on the desk, along with a lens cap for her camera, yesterday's mail, and the telephone book open to the yellow pages. Books, of course, were everywhere. Some were opened for reference, others closed, with bookmarks sticking out, mutely calling her back. The newspaper was folded on the coffee table along with a stack of magazines she hadn't had a chance to read.

Everything in the room was as warm and inviting as the woman sitting next to him, Brand decided. He acknowledged that he wanted all of that invitation and warmth for himself. Exclusive access.

Of course, there was the problem of overcoming his first disastrous impression, and that would take some doing. He'd never had Charlie's natural openness and social graces, but he didn't recall ever being quite so heavy-handed.

He'd spent too much time in the research lab these last few years, he brooded. He should have taken Charlie's advice to come out every other year or so and mingle with people, to speak a language other than computerese. Until he learned how to talk to Dena without putting his size eleven shoe in his mouth every time it was opened, the less said, the better.

Dena eyed the elegantly shod feet next to hers on the coffee table. Why didn't he say something, for heaven's sake, or had he come in just to drink Scotch and stare at the flames in the fireplace? Had he no conversation at all? She ordinarily didn't mind being with quiet people. They were restful, but something about Brand's silence paralyzed her tongue. Were they going to spend the rest of the evening together and never say a word?

"All evening I've wanted to take the pins out of your hair and watch it fall to your shoulders. Will you take it down?" Brand felt the words leave his mouth and closed his eyes in disbelief. My God! She'd think he was crazy.

Dena stared at the tanned remote profile. Had he really asked her... He had. Well, she was getting exactly what she deserved. She'd wanted him to say something and finally he had. Yes, indeed, he certainly had. She ought to have learned by now that when you ask, and receive, there's usually a zinger attached somewhere.

She hesitated, feeling a reluctance all out of proportion to the request. There was something symbolic about it, as if she would be lowering her guard as well as her hair. She caught a glint of challenge in the gleam of his eyes. Why not? she wondered recklessly. Why not let down her hair, literally as well as figuratively? She had allowed his silence to subdue her and that was ridiculous. And, after all, he did *ask*.

"All right."

Feeling a bit like a stripper facing her first audience, Dena raised her arms and felt for the pins.

Brand set his glass on the table and turned to watch.

Once again, Dena felt the pull of his gray eyes, and her fingers fumbled to a stop. His hand lifted and touched hers.

She felt the rumble of his voice as he said, "Let me."

He dropped the pins into her waiting hand, his eyes never leaving her sun-streaked mane as it fell in soft waves around her face.

Dena shook her head, as much to settle her hair as to break the spell that Brand's silent concentration had woven. His silence, as the man himself, had many facets. At the moment it was highly charged.

Brand's fingers brushed Dena's neck, sliding to cup her nape. Her move had been a strategic mistake, she thought wryly. All it had succeeded in doing was tangling his fingers in her hair, and somehow bringing him closer.

"It's silky," he murmured, his warm breath brushing her forehead. "And—" he drew in a deep breath "—it smells like...flowers."

A tremor shook her as his thumb grazed her earlobe. He felt it, of course. He might be quiet, but he wasn't slow! Without seeming to move, Brand pressed Dena back against the sofa.

"Must be the shampoo," she muttered prosaically, wiggling to gain some breathing space. "Or the conditioner. Or maybe the mousse."

His lips, which had progressed from her temple to cheekbone, drew to a startled halt. "No moose ever smelled this good," he said decisively, and resumed his leisurely exploration.

"Brand." Noting with annoyance that her voice was breathless, she cleared her throat and tried again. "Brand, I don't think—"

"Good," he murmured absently. "Don't."

She opened her eyes and jerked in shock as they met his. His pupils were enlarged and filled with a purpose and hunger she had never expected to see directed at her.

"Brand—"

His lips finally met hers, settling down as if they had come home. One hand cupped her head while the other found the curve of her waist. His arm tightened, drawing her soft body to the waiting hardness of his.

His lips were soft, testing, exploring, seeking an answer. When he found it, he drew her closer still. Dena's hands, which had risen to his shoulders in protest, halted briefly then moved on until they crossed at the back of his neck, her fingers kneading his taut muscles. She had anticipated a kiss that reflected the man, a bit cool and reserved, but had not expected to be swept away by the staggering sensuality of his touch.

Just as she realized that it had been some time since she had taken a breath, Brand raised his head and filled his lungs with air, his gaze never leaving her face. Their eyes met, and once again she was stunned by the expression in his. Hunger. It was the look of a ravenous man who had been handed an hors d'oeuvre and was now waiting for the main course.

She drew in a shuddering breath and hazily took stock of the situation. Just as she became aware that something had to be done, and was about to do it, Brand moved again.

He tightened his grasp on her, turned and leaned against the back of the sofa, taking her with him. Dena found herself with her head on his chest, listening to the rapid drumming of his heart. Her pulse rate rose to meet his when she realized that she was lying along his length, touching from toes to head.

He sighed with obvious contentment and rested his chin on the top of her head. One arm supported her waist while the other hand hypnotically smoothed the curve of her hip and thigh.

"God, you feel delicious. Don't move a muscle," he commanded in lazy satisfaction.

Surprised by the sudden reversal, Dena remained quiet. "That was a smooth move, McAllister," she managed finally. The words were a blend of wry amusement and accusation.

"I don't spend *all* my time in the lab," he said complacently.

That was an understatement if she ever heard one. He might not emerge very often, but he had obviously made good use of the times he did. She shifted restlessly, wondering if this reaction was unique or if he looked at every woman with eyes full of imminent starvation.

"What's the matter?" he asked in a quiet voice. "Why the sudden tension?"

"Nothing important," she hedged, wishing she hadn't thought about him with other women. For some mysterious reason, it seemed important. Reluctantly, she moved her legs. "Let me go, Brand."

"Right now?" His arms tightened instinctively.

"Yes." She waited in silence, wondering if she'd have to fight her way out of his embrace.

Once again he surprised her. His muscles slowly relaxed.

"For now," he agreed laconically. She knew it was both a promise and a threat. He fully intended to have her in his arms again, and she doubted if she'd be released so easily the next time.

Dena slid to the cushion beside him, leaving a wide buffer zone between them. She tugged at her blue wool skirt, covering her thighs and trying to smooth the wrinkled material. Deciding that it was time to tone down the charged atmosphere, she asked brightly, "So what's your master plan to plug the leak at Mitchell's?"

"I don't have one. Yet."

"Too bad you blew your chance to work with the resident genius. It would've made your job a lot easier."

"So what do you want, a written apology?"

"Not a bad idea," she said consideringly. "Of course, at this point, to satisfy my curiosity, I'd take anything written from you. Even a grocery list."

"A typed apology," he amended.

Suddenly serious, she asked, "And what would you say in this hypothetical apology?"

He eyed her warily.

"Would you tell me that you're sorry you offended me, but you still don't believe in what I do?"

"If I did say something along that line, what would your answer be?" he asked cautiously, is if he were treading his way through a mine field.

"That I understand your dilemma, but I only work with people who have faith in me," she answered promptly.

"Do you really understand?"

The intensity of the question revealed its importance.

"I think so." Now her voice was cautious.

"Enough to be objective about it?"

"Try me."

"Do you understand that I've spent most of my life working with a true science, with numbers and symbols? That they supply me with logical and precise answers? And, damn it, you're asking me to believe in something that relies on artistic interpretation and is still fighting for scientific recognition?"

"Let me ask you one," she said, after a thoughtful silence. "When you've worked on something in the past, has your imagination or instinct ever taken a quantum leap ahead? Has it said, 'I know this is way out in left field, but I'm sure it'll work,' and then you've gone back to your building blocks of mathematics and proven it?"

He stared at her in speechless fascination.

Her smile was slow and satisfied. "I rest my case."

Chapter Three

"Well, have you converted that nephew of mine yet?"

"Charlie? Charlie!" Dena gripped the telephone in disbelief at the sound of the familiar voice. "Where are you? *How* are you? Are you back already? You know what the doctor said about taking it easy."

A familiar chuckle rolled across the line. "Relax, honey. What should I answer first?"

"Start anywhere you want," she said in heady relief at hearing him sound so like himself.

"I'm on my boat, I'm fine, I'm not back and I remember every blasted word that killjoy said. What's even worse, so does my cook. Dena, you should see the stuff he gives me to eat."

"It's good for you," she said heartlessly. Despite his aggrieved tone, Charlie wasn't suffering. His boat was the last word in yachts, and his cook was a famous chef he had coaxed away from a four-star hotel. "So what are you up to?"

"Nothing," he said in disgust. "All there is out here is water."

"I heard from an impeccable source that boats are usually found near water."

"Don't be funny. Have you ever sat on one all day, soaking up sun and watching for flying fish?"

"Some people call that relaxing," she said dryly. "I understand that they even pay good money to do it."

"Now why did I think I might get some sympathy from you?" he wondered aloud. "I tell you my sad story and all I get is bad jokes."

"You don't deserve sympathy. You're lucky to be alive and you know it."

"I do know it," he agreed promptly. "But that doesn't keep me from being bored. I'm used to being busy."

"Charlie, what you need is a hobby."

"I had one," he said testily. "Two. But they won't let me fly or drive my racing car."

"Well, find another one."

"Like what?"

Dena grinned. He was really determined to be a grump. "What about photography?"

"Would you sit through a slide show of water and clouds?"

"How do you feel about crossword puzzles?"

His sound of disgust threatened her eardrum.

"I did have an idea," he said casually.

Dena sat up alertly. She'd heard that tone before. Usually when he was about to wheedle her into doing something.

"Oh?"

"How about coming out here to be with me for a while?"

Dena didn't answer immediately. She knew there was nothing more to the offer than appeared on the surface, but still she was surprised. Charlie was older than her father and treated her with the casual fondness he might show a niece. The rapport they found at their first meeting escalated when he discovered she shared his cutthroat approach to card games. They had spent many noisy evenings trading insults over her dining-room table.

"I could send a plane for you and we could play cribbage and pinochle. I'd even let you win every now and then."

"I can do that without your help," she retorted.

"Prove it."

"Nope, Charlie my love, it won't work. You're not going to goad me into flying God-knows-where just to prove what I already know. Sorry, but I've got a lot on my hands right now. I can't leave."

"What's so important that you can't come out and see a sick old man? Anything interesting going on?"

"Nothing that concerns you," she assured him hastily, ignoring his obvious ploy for pity. "Just the usual stuff, but lots of it."

"Have you met Brand yet?" he asked casually.

"Oh, yes, I've had the pleasure. Why didn't you warn me that you were leaving me in the hands of an unbeliever?"

Her teasing words evoked an image of hands cupping her face and bringing her closer—

"What did you say, Charlie? Sorry, I didn't hear you."

"I said you've got to get him out of that lab and warm him up a bit."

Warm him up? If his thermostat inched another degree higher, he'd go up in flames. She thought of the night before, when he had been leaving. She'd handed him his jacket and he had leaned against the door, looking at her.

"I'll be back, you know."

"You've got a lot of drinking to do," she joked lamely, wary of the unsettling look in his silvery eyes.

"There's only one thing bringing me back," he said bluntly. "You."

The pounding of her heart made such a commotion, she could hardly speak. "Brand," she managed, in full retreat, "I don't think you understand."

"Yes, I do," he said calmly. "Tonight I found a woman of warmth and passion. I want that fire. I'm coming back to claim it, and you." He leaned down, touching his lips to hers. "First step is tomorrow night. Dinner at six-thirty." His hands at her waist drew her to him and lifted until her feet left the ground and she was supported by his muscular frame. Her arms slid over his shoulders and settled around his neck. Minutes later, when he set her gently on her feet, she stood, flushed and breathless, watching as he stepped outside and silently closed the door.

No, Brand definitely didn't need warming up.

"Sorry, Charlie, I think we've got a bad connection," she lied. "I didn't hear you."

"I said something's got to get him out of that lab. I've done my part, the rest is up to you."

"What do you mean, me? He's not my responsibility."

"Well," he said reasonably, "you have to work with him for a year. You might as well make it easy on yourself."

"Why is he the one taking over for you? Couldn't it have been someone a little more—a little friendlier? I know he's your nephew, but—"

"He's the obvious one to do it," Charlie said in surprise.

"Why?"

"Because he's my partner."

"*What?*"

"He owns half of Mitchell's. I thought everyone knew that."

"Apparently everyone but me. I never hear his name connected with the company."

"Because he wants it that way. He doesn't like dealing with the media, and frankly, I'm just as glad. He's, ah, known more for his honesty than tact."

"I can believe that," Dena muttered.

"It's old news in the industry," Charlie continued. "My silent partner doesn't attract much attention, and that's just the way he wants it. We've always worked together in the lab, but he leaves all the outside contacts to me. Now, because of my blasted ticker, he's been thrown into the deep end overnight."

Dena tensed in the silence that followed.

"I hope," Charlie said slowly, "you'll be there for him if he needs you."

"That's a strange thing to say. Are you expecting trouble?" She frowned when he didn't respond immediately.

"Damn it!" he exploded. "I should be there instead of bobbing like a cork in the middle of the Indian Ocean."

"Why don't you tell me what's really bothering you, and maybe I can help," she said in a calm voice. It wasn't doing him a bit of good to go away if he was just going to worry about Brand, the new computer, the company, or anything else, she thought in concern. "Come on, Charlie, give."

"This is a critical time," he explained. "Right before a breakthrough, people are at their most vulnerable. They work long hours, they live on black coffee and cigarettes, and they don't get enough sleep. One minute their adrenaline is flowing and they're riding a false high and the next tempers are flaring out of control."

He cleared his throat. "Sometimes a key employee begins to estimate how much the company's going to make on this particular product. Then he looks at his take-home pay. Regardless of his salary, bonuses, or perks, it never seems enough. And believe me, we pay better than most companies, but there are always agents from competitors hanging around with more money in their pockets."

"Do you suspect that you have a weak link somewhere?"

"Possibly. Probably," he admitted realistically. "I don't know for sure that anything's wrong, but experience tells me that if something's going to happen, it'll be soon. In the past I've always been there, and I have a pretty good nose for stuff like that. Brand is different, though. Once he gets near the innards of anything electronic, he doesn't notice a thing. When he concentrates on something, he's totally absorbed."

"I've noticed," Dena said wryly, aware that she hadn't fully recovered from his undivided attention the night before.

"You told me once that your security people were the best. What about them?" She crossed her fingers behind her back. "If they're satisfied, isn't everything okay?"

"Honey," he said heavily, "you can have every security gadget in the world, and the best people, but *real* security lies in the basic integrity of each employee. And these days, you just never know." She could almost see him shaking his head at her naive question.

"Okay," she sighed, "if you'll promise to quit worrying, I'll promise to help."

"Good," he said with obvious relief. "With your background, you've got a feel for this sort of thing."

"What do you want me to do?"

"Just look around. Ask Brand for a tour of the lab. Get in there and meet the people. See what kind of vibes you pick up."

"And if I draw a blank?"

"I hope to God you do. But if there's anything going on, you'll feel it."

They talked for a few more minutes and Dena heard the tension leave his voice. As they were saying goodbye, she remembered something he had said earlier. "Wait a minute, Charlie. What are you doing in the Indian Ocean?"

"Damned if I know," he snorted. "I was so disgusted when I left I just told the captain to get moving and to keep going until he found something interesting."

Dena still had a smile on her lips when she replaced the receiver. It faded as she contemplated her rash offer. The horse she had climbed on was very high and it would take a contortionist to step down without breaking a leg.

She was still working on face-saving solutions when the telephone rang again.

"Hello."

"Ms Trevor?" There was no mistaking Brand's voice. She blinked at the buzzing formal greeting.

"Yes."

"The same one who has her master's in psychology and does counseling in the local school district?"

"You've been snooping!"

"You're right," he agreed grimly. "I went through Charlie's personal files." His voice was a curious blend of icy distance and simmering temper.

"Why are you so angry?"

"Why didn't you tell me?"

"Why should I? It has nothing to do with my job at Mitchell's."

"The hell it doesn't!"

"I was hired by Charlie," she said through gritted teeth, "as a graphoanalyst. Not as a psychologist, not as a counselor. Therefore, my degree has nothing to do with it or you."

"You still should have told me."

"Why?"

"Because it matters."

"I don't see why." Dena's frown of concentration grew darker as she groped to follow his thoughts. She didn't like where they were leading.

He muttered something about her not seeing her finger in front of her nose on a sunny afternoon, but she was too busy arriving at some conclusions to pay much attention.

"Wait a minute," she said slowly. "Are you by any chance trying to tell me that my skills as a graphoanalyst, which were still running a poor second to the Ouija board the last time we talked, are validated now because I have a degree in something?"

"It sure helps," he said clearly...and disastrously. He flinched at the soft and furious sound of her voice.

"Don't do me any favors, Mr. McAllister." It took all of her control to hang up quietly. She would rather have thrown the telephone on the floor and jumped on it.

It shrilled a summons before she moved from her desk. Even the bell sounded aggressive, she thought. Picking it up, she snarled, "What do you want now?"

"What in the hell is the matter with you?" His voice was so controlled it was almost a murmur. He didn't rant and storm when he was angry, she remembered. Apparently his voice lowered in direct proportion to his fury. If that was the case, he sounded ready to chew the legs of his walnut desk.

"I am angry," she said precisely. "Very angry."

"Even I figured that out," he said. "What I want to know is why."

"Because you needed the proof of a piece of paper, one that has no bearing on the situation, before you would believe that I could do my job."

"Is that all?" he asked in relief.

"All? *All?*" Why hadn't she throttled him the first time she thought about it? It would most certainly have been justifiable homicide. No jury, assuming it was composed of women, would ever convict her.

"I just made an important statement, Mr. McAllister. I'd advise you to think about it before you say anything else."

"Dena—" his voice was almost genial "—if you call me Mr. McAllister one more time, I'm going to come over to your place and you're going to lose the advantage of having several miles and a telephone wire between us. My name is Brand, B...r...a...n...d. Do you hear me, Dena?"

"I hear you," she said grudgingly.

"Good. Now where were we?"

"You were trying to figure out the importance of what I said," she told him coldly.

"You're dying to tell me, so why don't you just let me have it with both barrels?"

"All right," she snapped. "You have a certain reputation in your field. Let's pretend that I want something designed and you let me know you're available. But I doubt you're capable and let you know it. I finally tell you that you can use an office to put some squiggles on a piece of paper. In another office, however, I have another man also squiggling on paper, just in case you don't do it right. Then one day, while snooping in someone else's files, I find proof that you're an honest-to-

God, bona fide engineer. I tell you I now trust your squiggles and will get rid of the other man. And all because you are a graduate of engineering school. Just how flattered would you be?"

"You're forgetting the big difference between our work," he pointed out. "Everyone knows about my field, but how many have heard about yours?"

Dena all but gnashed her teeth. "Ten or fifteen years ago, you might have been right, but since then, articles in magazines and newspapers have educated the public. Anyone who doesn't know about it by now has probably had his head buried in a computer for the last five years."

"I don't know why you're so touchy about it. All I'm trying—"

"Touchy?" She rolled her eyes heavenward before closing them.

"You know, for someone who does a lot of counseling, you sure have a hair-trigger temper."

Dena recalled Charlie's words. The man was indeed more honest than tactful.

"Since you aren't a patient," she informed him, "I'm allowing myself the luxury of responding in a perfectly normal manner. And if that means losing my temper, then I'll damn well *lose it*."

"Fine," he said abruptly. "Lose it all you want. In fact, I hope it's completely gone by the time I pick you up for dinner."

"Dinner?"

"At six-thirty," he said implacably. "We arranged it last night, remember?"

"That was before you called me today."

"Dena, we may have differences about work, but that has nothing to do with us." His voice was as stubborn as his words.

"That may work for you, but I can't separate the two so easily."

"I'll show you how tonight," he promised. He hung up before she could answer.

Five hours later, Dena was still fuming. She had taken a long, warm bath to soothe away her annoyance. It hadn't worked. She had dressed in her favorite tweed pant suit to raise her spirits. That hadn't worked either. Deciding that she didn't want to eat at a restaurant, she made chicken, rice pilaf, glazed carrots and a green salad, raising a satisfying clamor with pots and utensils. All of the noise hadn't noticeably elevated her mood.

Now, waiting for Brand, she sat, flipping through the pages of a magazine, occasionally glancing out the window. She couldn't ever remember anyone irritating her the way he did. Why on earth did she let him get to her? Because he was an analytical, logical jackass, she answered promptly.

He's not that bad, and you know it, said the inner voice that never allowed her the luxury of making sweeping statements.

Yes, he is, she insisted stubbornly.

You're taking it out on him because you know you should be at the plant trying to match that writing.

That's not true.

Ha! If Charlie were here, you would have stayed yesterday morning.

Who could work with such a man? He's impossible.

He's allowed to have doubts. And the way he gets information is to ask questions.

Insulting ones!

Wrong. They're analytical, the same kind he would ask when approaching anything new. You're adding the emotion.

Well, maybe you're right, she admitted reluctantly. And maybe I could cope if that's all there was. But, have you seen the way he watches me? He practically undresses me with those gray eyes. He never looks away, hardly even blinks— *You're exaggerating again.*

—and he's too big. I can't breathe when he gets close. And when he kisses me— *You're scared!*

You're right!

Brand pulled up and parked in front of Dena's town house. He had spent the day with Jay Landry, head of Protective Services. It had been a frustrating day for both of them. The story was still the same. Information was getting out, and they didn't know who was doing it or how.

"I'm about ready to get everyone on the staff a four-leaf-clover and a rabbit's foot," Landry had finally grumbled. "We've tried everything else."

Brand was ready to go even further. At various times during the day he had considered a medicine man, a psychic, and...a graphoanalyst. The only problem, he admitted, was that he had alienated the most logical choice. Now, if he could just smooth her ruffled feathers—although why she should be upset just because he'd asked a few simple questions—maybe she'd be willing to try.

If she did agree he hoped she wouldn't ask why he had changed his mind, because he wasn't really sure he had. Brand had found a book on the subject and spent half the night reading. He was impressed with the years of research dedicated to the subject, but still had questions. They, apparently, would have to be shelved for the time being, or asked of someone else.

He stared through the windshield, fingers drumming on the steering wheel. They needed every bit of help they could get. If, by some stroke of luck, Dena came across the handwriting and identified it, this thing could be wrapped up before much more damage was done. He frowned, imagining the reaction he'd get if he asked for help. The range encompassed everything from stunned disbelief to outright laughter.

His frown deepened to a scowl as he considered his tentative handling of Dena. Dealing with such a proud and volatile woman had taught him one thing: the direct approach wouldn't work. He left the car and headed for her bright-blue door, whistling softly. He would have her at work before the week was out. And she would think it was her own idea.

Chapter Four

"Fifteen-two, fifteen-four, four is eight, and game."

"Damn!"

"That's two for me. Want to try for three out of five? You only have to win three straight games."

"You really know how to hit where it hurts, don't you?"

Dena eyed the cribbage board complacently. "My uncle taught me. His motto was 'no quarter asked, no quarter given.' If he left any gaps in my education, Charlie filled them in. Your uncle also cheats if he thinks he can get away with it."

Brand swept the cards toward him and shuffled expertly. "I must have left something out when I showed him how to play. Three out of five? Okay, let's go."

An hour later he moved his peg under Dena's indignant gaze and said "Game" for the third time.

"Are you sure you didn't cheat?"

"I don't have to," he mocked softly, grinning at her suspicious glare. "I do my best work under pressure."

She made a sound of muffled disgust and put the cards aside.

"What does the winner get?" Brand asked with interest.

"Victory," she said succinctly. "The sweet smell of success."

"That's all?"

"That's it. Unless you'd like to celebrate with a drink. Some generous soul brought over a bagful of stuff the other night. I don't think he'd mind if you helped yourself."

"Want a glass of wine?" He waited for her answer before turning to the kitchen.

"Please."

What a strange evening, Dena thought as she settled on the sofa and kicked off her gray-heeled sandals. Brand had been startled then pleased to be confronted with home-cooked food. The meal itself had been punctuated with thoughtful lapses of conversation and, occasionally, extended silence. Dena was curious about Brand's abstracted air. She knew only too well what caused her own. Her promise to Charlie weighed heavily on her conscience.

If she practiced what she preached in her counseling sessions about being open and avoiding game-playing, she would simply tell Brand that even if he didn't believe in her work, she'd like to go to the plant and see if she could help. But, God help her, she was *not* being mature or open about it. The man drove her nuts and, to retaliate, she was indulging in a bit of manipulative face-saving. It's one thing to do it and not know when you're doing it; that's when it's bad, she told herself. But, if you do it, and you *know* you're doing it— *It's even worse,* dryly commented her inner voice, which, besides disliking sweeping statements, had a thing about rationalizing.

Oh, be quiet, she told her conscience. Even if my method is a bit roundabout, I'll work it out. Somehow, I'll get into the plant and maneuver my way into a cubbyhole near personnel. I'll keep my promise, and also show that stubborn pragmatist a thing or two.

She heard the clink of glass on crystal and the refrigerator door close. It was still early. Far too early for him to think of leaving. He had spied the cribbage board while they were clearing the dishes from the table and asked if she played. She had agreed, hoping to avoid any more awkward silences. It had worked, for a while. Now what? she wondered. They were both obviously treading carefully, avoiding potentially dangerous subjects. But as their work and all peripheral areas fell into that category, it limited them to the very personal or inane. She sighed. Nothing was simple.

Brand placed the drinks on the oak and glass coffee table, carefully avoiding the wood. He sat beside her as if there was no other furniture in the room. Dena edged away from the touch of his thigh, tucked her feet under her, and turned to face him, propping an elbow on the back of the sofa. He half turned, reached for his glass, and leisurely studied her face.

Aware that the full blast of his concentration was turned on her, Dena felt a warmth rushing up from some inner well and radiating out to her fingertips. When some men looked, they did a blatant sizing up, others were more subtle, but still obvious. They were easy enough to cope with. Brand's silent regard was more difficult to handle. It was a calm inspection that slowly became appreciative. It seemed to absorb her fragrance, to taste the very essence of her. It was, she decided, enough to fill a woman with trepidation, not to mention anxiety and apprehension. She broke the spell by reaching for her glass.

"I'm curious," Brand said abruptly. "Haven't you ever wanted to see the layout at the company?"

"I did at first, but Charlie wanted me to stay a well-kept secret. And it really doesn't matter," she assured him. "I can work anywhere. In fact, my office is here in the house."

"I'd like to see it," he said. "Would you mind?"

"Not at all." She rose and led him back to the entry hall. "But there's nothing exciting about it. It's just a bedroom turned into an office."

It was more than that, Brand decided, much more. The hallway was banked with several indoor trees and baskets of greenery. It was designed to lead either into the living area or the office.

"Nice touch," he said, standing at the front door and realizing that his eye had previously led him directly into the living room. Now that she was indicating the way, he saw that there was also a natural invitation into the office area. "Did you do it yourself?"

"With some help from a friend who's a professional decorator."

The office was warm and welcoming. The carpet was a muted rust. The shade was repeated on one wall, lending a colorful background to a variety of framed certificates and diplomas. Two opposing walls had floor-to-ceiling bookshelves. Books and plants covered almost every available space, he noted. At the end of each wall a ladder was propped, giving access to even the highest shelf. Two floral, high-backed chairs were placed at a comfortable angle before the focal point of the room, a large fruitwood desk. A magnifier lamp was mounted on one corner, its severity broken by a basket of trailing greenery. Two filing cabinets were painted cream to match the last wall. It was a room of space and light.

"What's that for?" Brand indicated the fluorescent lamp with the magnifying lens.

"That's as necessary to my work as a calculator is to yours."

"The only resemblance between your office and the one I have at home is the number of books. I work in complete chaos," he admitted.

"That doesn't fit your image," she commented, closing the door and leading the way back to the living room. "You seem extraordinarily neat."

"I am. Everywhere else." He waited politely for her to be seated, then promptly lowered himself next to her.

Dena used the pretext of reaching for her glass to edge away a few inches. She always seemed to be backing away from him, she thought. He obviously wasn't concerned about people intruding on

his personal space. Strangely enough, she normally didn't think about it much either, except
where he was concerned.

She could feel the tension building between them
and wondered how he could appear to be so relaxed. Why didn't he just pounce and get it over
with? Pouncing she could handle, it was the waiting that drove her crazy. Fire, he had called it. Said
he would return to claim it, and her. Well, here they
were, just the two of them. What the devil was he
waiting for? She couldn't decide if she was disap-
pointed or relieved. One thing she knew for certain, she was exhausted. Being on guard all evening,
she reflected, especially when it was unnecessary,
was hard work.

He finished his drink and leaned forward to set
his glass on the table. She jumped, her wine sloshing in the glass, as he turned to her.

"You know what you mentioned earlier," she
said impulsively, cutting off whatever he intended
to say, "about visiting the plant? I'd really like to,
unless you think Charlie is right and I should stay
away."

Dena couldn't decipher the varied expressions
that flickered in Brand's eyes, but she had the uneasy suspicion that satisfaction was one of them.
He leaned back against the sofa and presented her
with his profile, so she couldn't be sure.

His voice was casual. "I don't see any problem.
Come on down and I'll give you the fifty-cent
tour."

"When?"

"Why not tomorrow?"

"Aren't you busy right now plugging leaks?"

"No, tomorrow's fine. About ten?"

"Fine," she said slowly, still surprised at his prompt response.

"Good. We'll go to lunch afterward if you have time."

She found herself agreeing, rising with him and watching as he put on his jacket. He leaned down, placed a hard kiss on her soft lips and opened the door.

"Ten sharp," he reminded her, and turned away.

Dena told herself bracingly that she was glad he was leaving without a skirmish. And she was definitely not feeling disgruntled. The surprising thing was, it didn't fit his personality. She had expected more...persistence, more determination. But she was pleased, she assured herself hastily. Very pleased.

She also had a niggling feeling that she'd been had. Brand looked far too satisfied as he walked to the curb, whistling softly as he tossed his keys in the air, catching them on the downward swing.

She was still brooding the next morning as she turned into Mitchell's industrial parkway. Absently admiring the beautiful landscaping, she drove past the track and athletic area installed for joggers and fitness enthusiasts. The parking lots were surrounded by masses of trees, most of which were turning various shades of gold, bronze, and red. To anyone driving by, the entire area resembled an inviting park rather than an industrial complex.

Dena parked the car in the visitors' area, was checked through various security stations, and delivered to Brand's office. Her clothing was a cheerful contrast to the olive drab uniform of her escort from Protective Services. She had chosen her favorite suit, a subtle red and gray plaid. A red blouse, purse and shoes completed the outfit. In it she felt ready for anything. And 'anything' was exactly what she might encounter, because she had decided to grasp whatever opportunity came her way. Even though it was Friday, this was the day to start fulfilling her promise to Charlie. Actually, she had begun last night, staring at her bedroom ceiling, formulating stories to cover her sudden appearance at the plant.

"Good morning, Miss Trevor. Mr. McAllister will be with you in a moment." Brand's secretary had also manned the desk when Charlie occupied the inner office.

"Thank you, Mrs. Hastings, I'm in no hurry."

Indeed not, Mrs. Hastings. I'm not a bit anxious to meet the man who continually throws me off balance and gives me the uneasy feeling that he's up to something. With a sense of reprieve, Dena sat down and picked up a magazine. She gazed raptly at the meaningless jumble of print about new high-tech development in the computer field.

She knew why she was there, but why was Brand taking time out of an obviously busy schedule to show her around? He had his hands full just in combining Charlie's responsibilities with his own. Add to that the theft of information, and you had *twenty-four hour workday. It just didn't make
        "Sorry I'm late." Brand's crisp voice
    *r confused meandering. "Ready?"

She rose in answer. "Where do we go first?" she asked briskly, brushing away her doubts.

"Have you ever seen the inner workings of security?"

"Nope. I've never known anyone with enough clout who wanted me to."

"Then this is your lucky day," he informed her. His warm hand touched the small of her back as he ushered her out the door.

"Exactly why am I so privileged?"

"One, you're no security risk and two, because we've run out of ideas and you just may come up with something."

The amazing power of a degree, she thought wryly. Because I have that piece of paper, I'm now qualified to have ideas, even some that might work!

They went down several floors in the elevator, wound through a series of halls that were remarkable only for their similarity, and stopped at a door indicating it housed Protective Services. Brand slipped his plastic badge into a slot by the door and stood aside as it opened. They stepped inside and it closed silently behind them.

A tall, thin man in his forties, who looked like he ran on nervous energy, glanced up from a bank of television monitors. Even though he was sitting, he was in constant motion. Flicking off one screen and turning on another, he drummed a tattoo on the table while it focused.

"Knew you'd be along any minute now," he drawled.

Dena's gaze, which had settled on the monitors, jerked to him in surprise. She had expected a machine gun spate of words to match his restless movements. It was such inconsistencies that fascinated her.

Brand's voice murmured introductions and she found herself shaking hands with Jay Landry. "He's the head honcho around here," Brand added.

"For my sins," Jay agreed morosely. "Why I ever went into such a thankless line of work, I'll never know." He ran a hand through a mane of silver-shot brown hair and scowled at the monitors. "Will you just look at that," he muttered in disgust. "Not a soul where he shouldn't be, and everyone looks as innocent as a morning glory."

He turned a mobile face to Dena. "Hear you're the local shrink. Got any ideas about this mess?"

Her expression lightened at his tone of amiable commiseration. "I just found out that I was supposed to have some. Before I get clever, why don't you tell me what this—" she gestured to the screens "—is all about?"

He pointed a bony finger at several on the end. "Parking area," he said laconically.

Dena looked closely at the columns of parked cars on the screen. "Do you only get an overview?"

He punched a button and she watched as the monitor zoomed in on one car until she could see through the rear window. "Nope. We can get close enough to count a gnat's eyelashes if we want to." He flipped a switch and followed a car through the parking lot.

"How far is your camera range?" she asked with interest.

"We cover the entire complex, inside and out."

"The whole thing?"

"Almost. All the important areas. All the exits and roadways.

"If you had to, could you stop someone leaving?"

He pointed again, this time to a red telephone. "Direct hook up to the police." He nodded at another screen. "Security cars parked out in front with the keys in the ignition. Always ready. If we don't get roadblocks up in time, we could keep in radio contact with the police and follow the car until the police pick it up."

She watched people coming and going on the other screens. "What's all that?"

"Hot spots in the building." He nodded to the center ones. "That's the R and D lab where the trouble's brewing. Research and Development," he added, noting her puzzled expression. "We run twenty-four hour tapes and have someone review them each day."

She looked at the five people on the screen with curiosity. Two women and three men were standing by a desk, each clutching a handful of papers. Even to an outsider, it was obvious that they were torn by disagreement.

"Those are the engineers I've had working with me on the new computer," Brand murmured to Dena, watching the monitor intently. "Jay, I took your suggestion and changed the work schedule. Until this mess is straightened up, I'm the only one working it. I've switched them all to other phases. Turn the sound up," he directed the older man. "I want to listen."

Dena opted for observation rather than trying to make sense of the conversation. The younger woman was giving short, unencouraging nods to whatever the older man was saying. She was obviously just waiting to dazzle him with some bit of information. The other two men, both a few years younger than Brand, were aligned against the older woman. There wasn't one of them actually listening to another, Dena noted without surprise.

"That's enough," Brand said wearily. "It's the same old thing. They all think that their own ideas are the only ones that work."

He dropped his arm around Dena's shoulders. "We've still got a lot of ground to cover. We'd better be on our way." He looked at the other man. "Thanks for staying to meet Dena, Jay."

"My pleasure." He nodded at Dena then gestured to the monitors. "I don't get to play with these very often. Sergeant Daniels has all the fun around here. She'll be back from her break in a few minutes. Oh, Dena." His voice was just a shade too casual and Dena looked back from the door where Brand had led her. "That tape running in R and D is confidential." The laconic mask was replaced by sharp intelligence for a questioning moment before it slid back in place.

Dena nodded and was hustled out the door by Brand. She waved in assurance to the other man just as it closed.

"Where now?" she asked, pulling at his arm to slow him down.

"Have you seen Personnel?"

"Only John's office."

"We'll do a quick walk through and then go up to some of the labs." He pressed the Up button for the elevator.

They waited in silence and Dena decided to keep an eye open for an empty desk or office in the area. She hadn't yet determined how to wiggle her way in, but by this time tomorrow, she promised herself, she'd be working there.

But all of the desks were occupied, and the doors leading from the main office were closed. Her resolution seemed destined for failure until hope, in the form of John Salcedo, strolled into view. A look of pleasure in his dark eyes, he directed his steps toward them. He murmured a casual greeting to Brand and smiled at Dena.

"I was going to call you later. I might not make it by six-thirty. I've got a meeting that might run late."

"The later you are, the hungrier I get," she warned with a grin. "And the more it costs you."

"That's what I get for dating a woman with a hearty appetite. Whatever happened to the ones who live on lettuce leaves and celery sticks?"

"They only do that when they're at home. They save all their calories for the nights that someone takes them out to dinner."

"Well, at least now I know," he said philosophically. "I thought they were a disappearing breed."

The exchange hadn't taken a minute, but it was more than enough time to put Brand in a foul mood. He scowled at John's retreating back, startled at the tension that unexpectedly invaded his body. He didn't want anyone else wining and dining Miss Dena Trevor. He also objected to anyone else dancing with and kissing her. The first was bad enough, but since he had held her in his arms and kissed her, and felt her surprising response to him, the latter was intolerable. Yes, he made a mental note, he'd have to do something about that.

Dena, unaware of her companion's grim expression, waved blithely as John left. He was a nice man, she decided for the hundredth time, and if all else failed, he might find her a spare cubbyhole to work in. No bells rang when they were together, for either of them, but they had fun. They liked to dance and were entertained by the same things. As a result, the occasional evenings they spent together were ones of ease and laughter. Against her will, she found herself comparing them with the times spent with Brand. No, John did not, thank God, fill her with caution and awkwardness. He did not keep her on the edge of her seat wondering what was going to happen next. He was a nice, charming, uncomplicated man.

Dena slanted a look up at Brand and was stunned by the black frown he directed at her. *Now* what was the matter? She hadn't said a word to annoy him. Not this time. If he were any other man, she thought, his scowl might be attributed to jealousy. She took another peek and bit back a grin. Possible, she decided, just possible. Before she could be sure, he disciplined his expression and moved on. She had the feeling that whatever had happened, it was the end of a promising morning. Then in sudden annoyance she drew to a stop, slipped her arm from his grasp, and tilted her head in a challenging manner.

"Where now?" she asked calmly, ignoring his sudden change.

He shot her a quick, assessing glance before answering. Taking a moment to cage the possessive animal he hadn't even known existed within himself, he said briefly, "Upstairs, to the labs."

In the next forty minutes, whatever had possessed him disappeared. This was his turf. His explanations were lucid and tinged with excitement. He regarded a piece of testing equipment with the pride another man might display when showing off his new baby. Dena looked at it, genuinely intrigued. What was it about this hunk of metal that warmed his gray eyes and sparked such enthusiasm in this self-contained man?

Two different worlds, she decided. That's what we live in. Mine is filled with people and their feelings. His is full of equations, equipment, tests, and responses. He'd spend hours over a drawing board, then with seemingly endless patience test one theory after another. She visualized him scowling at any two-footed specimen who dared to interrupt his train of thought. She, on the other hand, spent the same number of hours with people or their writing samples, dealing with foibles and idiosyncracies that would drive Brand mad. As far as machines and inanimate objects residing in her household were concerned, at any given time they had exactly thirty seconds to work correctly before they were threatened with destruction! Yes, their worlds were far apart.

Brand looked at his watch, halting his words of praise for yet another piece of machinery that looked, to Dena's uneducated eye, suspiciously like the previous ones. "One last stop before lunch," he promised. Opening the door, he gestured to his right.

Dena followed Brand through another door and stopped in her tracks. The five people had only moved about three feet from the desk and were still vociferously disagreeing. They broke off at the sight of Brand and surged toward him like an untidy wave aiming for the beach. Dena had a vague feeling of familiarity which had nothing to do with seeing them earlier on the television monitors.

"Brand, if you'd only look at these figures—"

"I told Art that we should eliminate—"

"I think I've figured out—"

"It's absolute nonsense—"

"Remember yesterday that I—"

Of course, she thought, biting her lower lip to restrain a grin. They all had the same formidable power of concentration—that single-minded devotion to the subject at hand. She wondered idly if it was in the genes, or a discipline acquired through their studies. Brand, she noted, was meeting fire with fire. He had obviously brought her in to meet them, and he ruthlessly broke through their harried comments.

"Dena, I'd like you to meet—"

It was a good attempt, considering his competition, but the wave had not yet crested.

"—I compiled this morning—"

"—the third function key—"

"—a new way to approach—"

"—that we should have to be—"

"—said that I thought we should—"

Dena looked around the circle of faces and back at Brand, arching her brows. The small tussle ended abruptly when Brand raised his voice.

"No," he said decisively.

All five of them ground to a stop.

"No, what?" The young, dark-haired woman finally asked.

Gray eyes shared a fleeting amusement with hazel ones.

"That's one word they always hear," Brand explained. "Now that I have your attention, I'd like to finish this introduction. Dena, meet Art Dexter, Mary Crowder, Wayne Randall, Karen Michaels, and Burt Silver."

It was like one of those awful brainteasers found in crossword-puzzle books, Dena decided. The type she always avoided. The kind that began "If Mr. Green lives in the blue house and Mr. Blue lives in the Green house" and only got progressively worse. Burt Silver did not have silver hair, but Art Dexter did. Mary Crowder was in her midforties with dyed red hair. Karen, obviously, was the younger woman with dark hair. That left two men. Both were about her age. One was slim and dark, the other was a blond Adonis with a mustache and a profile any male model would kill for.

"This is Dena Trevor," Brand continued. He placed a large, warm hand on her shoulder and drew her infinitesimally closer.

She glanced up in surprise. This was not your plain, ordinary, business-type introduction, she reflected. She had a moment to wonder exactly what he was up to before she found out.

"Dena's coming to work for us. Aren't you, darling?"

Chapter Five

W hy...yes. I am," she all but purred, sifting through her cover stories and pulling out the least improbable one. "In Personnel."

Her brilliant smile was directed at the five clustered around them. "I suppose I should say *with* you, not for. You see," she said chattily, "I work for a foundation that's doing a study on the correlation of competitive high-tech positions and stress-related health problems. Your company answered the foundation's plea for cooperation. So I'll be around for a while studying personnel and insurance documents."

"You're not an engineer?" one of the two unidentified men asked.

She shook her head in a negative reply. There was a visible show of disinterest, and five pairs of eyes drifted to papers held in five separate hands.

Brand's hand tightened on her shoulder. "We're going to be late for our lunch appointment." His voice promised retribution.

Resisting the pressure of Brand's hand as it dropped to the small of her back, Dena said her goodbyes, taking one last stab at remembering if Mr. Silver lived under the dark hair or the blond. Inwardly conceding defeat, she turned, smiled at Brand's square chin, and declared, "I'm ready anytime you are, *darling*."

As the door closed behind them, he said tersely, "I suppose you're pleased with yourself."

"Relatively," she admitted.

The drive to the restaurant was quick and silent.

Dena chose a spinach salad and tea and leaned back while Brand ordered a more substantial meal and got rid of the waiter. He turned back to her, a muscle twitching in his cheek.

"You're going to grind your teeth down to stubs," she said calmly. "You'd better get it off your chest."

"Why'd you do it?" he asked. He reached for his napkin and glared at it as if he wished it were her neck, and that he could wring it instead of merely placing it in his lap.

"Wait just a darn minute." She didn't try to hide her exasperation. "That's my line. You started the whole thing, and I'd like to know why."

"You're not going to like my answer," he countered.

She sighed. "I rarely do."

"We're grasping at straws now and I thought—"

"That since I'm the only straw in the water, you might as well grab?"

"Something like that."

Why doesn't he lie, she wondered indignantly. If he had any grace at all, he'd say that he's been unutterably stupid, he now recognizes my skill, as well as talent, that he begs my pardon and, as long as he's begging, won't I please come and find the thief? She brooded darkly on his lapse until his voice brought her back to the present.

"Why'd you do it?" he repeated.

"Because Charlie's worried," she answered promptly.

He raised startled brows. "How do you know?"

"Because he told me."

"Told you?"

"On the phone," she said succinctly. "The other night."

"How—"

She swallowed a mouthful of salad. "Don't ask me. I don't understand how telephones work on dry land with telephone poles all around, much less in the middle of the Indian Ocean."

"Radio," he said obscurely.

She waited for him to continue, but he seemed to think he had clearly explained the matter.

"That's not what I was going to say." He stared into his steaming cup of coffee, then raised his gaze to meet hers. "How does he know there's anything to worry about?"

"Gut instinct. And experience."

His voice grew as grim as the look in his eyes. "I can't make any sense of a conversation that starts in the middle. Would you mind going back to the beginning and tell me why he called? What did he want?"

"Me," she said cheerfully.

His brows shot up to his hairline before he rearranged them to glare at her.

"To fly out to meet him," she expanded. Popping a forkful of salad in her mouth, she chewed at length and finally admitted, "To play cribbage."

"I don't believe it," he muttered around a piece of broccoli.

She raised her right hand. "Scout's honor. He's bored with all the water." Growing serious, she gave him a judiciously edited version of their conversation. "I could see he was getting upset, so I promised I'd drop in and snoop around."

"You didn't tell him—"

"Give me credit for having a few brains. Of course I didn't."

Brand nodded an acknowledgment then reworded his original question. "Why didn't you just tell me you wanted to come down and work?"

"For the same reason you cornered me in front of your five paper-waving friends. I didn't want my words thrown back in my teeth. I'd done a terrific job of burning my bridges, but I was too mad to apologize. I figured I could weasel in one way or another. If all else failed, I was going to work on John tonight."

As soon as she uttered the words, she wished them back. Brand's disapproval was obvious.

"John," he repeated thoughtfully. "Do you see much of him?"

"Some." She hoped that her brief answer would close the subject.

"Are you sleeping with him?"

"*What?*"

"I said," he enunciated clearly, "are you—"

"Will you keep your voice down!" she muttered in a furious undertone.

"I thought you didn't hear me."

"You thought no such thing."

"Well?"

"Well, what?"

"Are you sleeping with him?" His dogged tone informed her that he wouldn't give up until he received an answer.

Persistent as well as literal, she decided with disgust. She wondered what his reaction would be if she replied in the affirmative, then decided that she didn't want to know badly enough to try it.

"No. Not that it's any of your business." She glared up at him, disliking the fleeting look of satisfaction that crossed his face.

"You know it is," he reminded her tersely. "I said I was coming back for you. Or did you forget?"

She refused to answer on the grounds that silence was the least incriminating of her options. Crazy man. How could any woman forget something like that? But he wasn't breaking any speed records doing it. Not that she wanted him to, she assured herself. The last thing in the world she needed was the man attaching himself to her, analyzing her every mood with the stubborn intelligence that was such a part of him. Especially since she had learned just how crazily she reacted to the touch of his arms and lips. No, the less he knew about that, the better off she'd be.

"About my new job in personnel," she began briskly.

Assuming that his grunt was as much acknowledgment as she would get, she enumerated her requirements, counting them off on her fingers as she went.

"First, I need an office. A small one will be fine," she assured him hastily. "Then, access to the files, of course. If you don't want to bother about that, I'll discuss it with John tonight. A telephone would help, but it isn't necessary."

Tapping a neatly shaped, pink fingernail on the table, she continued. "I can bring my own supplies, but a small dolly or cart to move the files would come in handy. I could work right out at the filing cabinets. Would that be too obvious, or did my story cover that? What do you think?" she prodded Brand, who seemed lost in some inner contemplation.

"If you're not sleeping with him, who are you sleeping with?" he asked.

Sheer fury hazed her vision for a moment. When it cleared, she was eyeing her utensils, wondering which one would inflict mortal damage. She removed her hand from the tempting weapons and glared at him.

"Did you hear anything I said?" she ground out.

"I was thinking," he said simply. "But maybe I should rephrase the question."

"Maybe you should forget it altogether!"

"Are you sleeping with anyone?"

"If you're not careful," she warned him, "the ten o'clock news is going to center around a berserk psychologist who stabbed her companion with a fork."

Not to be sidetracked with such frivolity, he persisted. "Are you?"

"Is it asking too much for you to elevate your thoughts a little higher than a mattress?"

"Are you?"

Inhaling deeply, she closed her eyes. In the past, she had dealt with engineers and other scientists, admiring their ability to concentrate, envying their intelligence. She had never been confronted with one of them on a personal basis. Now she understood why the divorce rate was so high in Silicon Valley. What reasonable woman could live with a man who concentrated so deeply that he was oblivious of his present surroundings and, worst of all, ignored her conversation? Especially if he was capable of repeating the same question with all the persistence of water dripping on a rock?

"I am not sleeping with anyone." The icy words were delivered slowly and emphatically.

"Good." He carefully placed his fork on his plate and covered her agitated hand with his. Turning it over, he brushed the tip of his finger across her palm. Shivering with reaction, she almost missed his next words.

"That takes care of now. What about before?"

Hot with renewed anger, she tugged at her hand and said, "What went on before we met has nothing to do with you!"

His surprised tone stopped her momentarily. "Of course it does. If you had been sleeping with someone, he may still think he has a claim on you."

"So?"

"I'll have to tell him things have changed."

Angry words tripped from her tongue with disastrous speed and clarity. "Once and for all, Brand McAllister, I am not now sleeping, nor have I ever—"

She stopped, appalled at her impetuous admission. She might be—and probably was, she decided gloomily—the last twenty-six-year-old virgin in the state of California, but she didn't have to proclaim it to the world or to the man sitting across from her.

"Ever what?" he urged softly, with the satisfied and slightly astonished look of a man who had come upon buried treasure when he least expected to.

"Nothing," she mumbled. "Look, are you almost through? I've got to get home. I have a lot of work piled up."

"Won't be long," he promised. He finished eating in thoughtful silence, and she stared fixedly at the remaining tea in her cup.

Six hours later, Dena was still castigating herself. Idiot! Of all the things to say to him. She should probably be grateful for his silence, that he didn't go into his Chinese water torture routine, but her instinct told her that where Brand McAllister was concerned, silence was not to be equated with forgetfulness. Besides, she reminded herself, he was no fool. He knew exactly what she had intended to say.

A glance at her watch informed her that John would soon be ringing the bell. Reaching into the closet, she brought out a red crepe dress that easily slid over her head. It was more of a problem to work the zipper up the back, but well worth the effort, she decided. Nodding at her reflection in the mirror, she eyed the plunging neckline and the way the dress clung to her curves. John would be surprised. When she dated him, she never wore anything that murmured such a seductive invitation. But it did wonders for her morale and, at the moment, that was all she was concerned about.

She quickly brushed her hair and let it fall to her shoulders. Clipping on earrings, she decided that any more jewelry was unnecessary. She was checking her small bag for keys and lipstick when the chimes sounded.

"You're not late, after all," she informed him, as she threw open the door. "Oh my God," she breathed in a tone of doom, as Brand's lean height filled the doorway. "What are you doing here?"

"John had something unexpected come up. I told him I'd stand in for him tonight." Brand stepped forward and she found herself instinctively retreating.

"You don't have to do that," Dena said politely, trying to be philosophical about his lingering assessment of the flaming dress.

His formal courtesy outdid her own. "It's my pleasure. It would be a shame for you to sit at home when you're obviously dressed for a big evening." His smooth, sarcastic tone was no more palatable than the dark looks he continued to cast at her dress.

Her options, Dena reflected, were limited. She could either get rid of him or get some food in his stomach and hope that his mood improved. The first was not viable, she decided, after taking in his determined stance. He had suddenly assumed the look of a man whose shoes were nailed to the floor. So it had to be food, and the sooner the better. Once that was done, she could concentrate on saying good-night at the door.

"I'll get my coat," she said abruptly, ignoring his look of surprise. Obviously he hadn't expected her to agree so readily.

"What do you say about going to Leo's?" she asked as he held her coat.

"Aren't you a little overdressed?"

"Not at all. He likes his patrons to get gussied up. Says it adds class to the place."

As they walked to the racy looking car, she asked, "Did you choose the color?"

"Of the car? Of course."

"Why red?"

"Why not? I like red."

Interesting, she thought. When she first met him, she would have sworn his car would be a conservative model, possibly a silver gray. Now, the glimpses she was getting of the man disclosed unexpected facets and most of them surprised her.

When they were seated in the restaurant, after Dena had been enveloped in an enthusiastic hug and listened while Leo spoke swiftly in Italian, she looked up from the menu to see Brand glowering at her dress.

Taking the battle into his camp, she commented, "I thought you liked red."

He seemed to bite off his words as he answered, "I do."

"Then you don't like my dress."

"Yes, I do," he said flatly. "And so does every other man in the room, especially your friend, Leo. I suppose he was telling you about his sister again?" His tone indicated that even if she swore on a stack of Bibles, he wouldn't believe an affirmative reply.

"Not exactly," she murmured, seeking refuge behind the large menu. Leo had, in fact, issued what she considered to be a grossly exaggerated warning. But if Brand's mood was any indication, perhaps she should take heed of the whispered words.

Leo had indicated that she was playing with fire, wearing such a dress while with a man who was so openly possessive. Her first reaction had been one of denial. Brand didn't own her. She knew it, he knew it, and there was no reason for anyone to think he did. But now, watching him, she was reminded of a large, alert dog who clearly believed that anyone within a square mile was planning to abscond with his favorite bone. His rumbling growl and show of gleaming canines would be just as effective as Brand's aura of taut competence. No one would mess with him!

"I think I'll try the veal," she said. Leaning back in her chair, she waited quietly while he placed the order. The wine, she noted, was a Riesling.

"Did you ask John if he has an office that I can use for a few days?"

He nodded. "He does. I'm sure that I don't have to tell you how pleased he is. One of the things he's doing tonight is running a computer list of all personnel working in that area. He'll have someone start pulling their files first thing Monday morning."

"Thank you."

He nodded again, a mocking inclination of his dark head that irritated her beyond belief. The waiter providentially interrupted by placing a tureen of soup between them.

"Tell me, Brand," she began as she dished up the aromatic concoction, "what do you do for amusement?"

"Lately, I've been taking stubborn, difficult, and enchanting women out to dinner," he observed blandly, his hand not even faltering as he raised the spoon to his mouth.

"Interesting. Which of the three do you find most compatible?" Her amber gaze was noticeably cooler.

"Each of them has her attraction, of course. But the one I've been concentrating on lately is a combination of all three. She's...intriguing, a bit like an equation. Just about the time I think I have all the unknowns isolated, another piece of data presents itself."

"Interesting," she murmured again, lying through her teeth. She knew damn well what bit of information had most recently presented itself! She waited with seething impatience for the waiter to whisk away the soup bowls and toss the salad. Her voice matched the temperature of her gaze as she asked, "Does that help solve the problem?"

"Not at all," he assured her, nodding in approval as he tasted the salad. "It merely increases the unknowns, and adds to the fascination."

If Charlie could hear this conversation, Dena decided grimly, he would know his worries were groundless. Brand had emerged from his lab with a vengeance. He was not only a force to be dealt with in the business world, he was an outright menace on the social level.

"Actually," she persevered, "I was thinking of hobbies. Do you have any?"

He silently considered her question. "Most of what I do is to keep in shape," he admitted. "I run, swim, lift weights, and play tennis when I have the time."

It figured. Most of it was competitive. If he didn't have an opponent, he would compete with himself, she mentally wagered. He probably ran with a stopwatch in one hand, somehow timed his laps, regularly increased his number of bench presses and played murderous tennis.

"Why?" He eyed her with genuine interest. "Are you going to take me in hand, show me how to have fun?"

"It sounds like someone should." It had become more than an idle question, she was really curious now. "What *do* you do for amusement?"

His silence was an eloquent admission. He finally broke it by saying, "I spend a lot of hours in the lab. My work is fascinating. I don't need much outside entertainment."

She nodded in understanding. "I can see how spending sixteen hours a day at work and the rest devoted to running, swimming, or throwing heavy things around wouldn't leave you much time for anything except sleep. But does any of that make you laugh?"

"Laugh?"

He made it sound as if he'd never heard of the word. Influenced by some emotion she couldn't immediately identify, she led the conversation into a less controversial direction. "Never mind. I was being more curious than polite. How's your chicken?"

"Fine," he said absently. His silvery gaze enmeshed with hers, swirling with challenge. "Did you make your point? If you did, it went over my head."

"No, I took pity on you and dropped the subject."

He shook his head. "I don't know what your success ratio is with your counseling patients, but if you give up that easily, it must be pretty low. You're too soft, lady."

Why had she thought he merited even an ounce of sympathy? He was clearly impossible. He was also an argumentative and insensitive clod!

"I told you once before," she said with determined patience, " you're not a patient and, difficult as it is, I'm trying to treat you as I would any other peer."

"But you were leading up to something," he persisted, "and I want you to finish."

"All right! God knows I wouldn't want to give you something else to add to your list of unknowns." She frowned, then demanded, "What kind of films do you prefer to watch?"

"Documentaries," he answered promptly.

"It figures," she retorted, momentarily putting aside her own partiality for them. "About vanished civilizations and dying animal kingdoms, I suppose?''

"Among others."

Dena eyed him narrowly. If she didn't know better, she would swear there was a glimmer of humor in his eyes.

"What about science fiction pictures?"

"I go to sleep after the first five minutes."

"*What?* How on earth can you do that?"

"I'll probably regret saying this," he decided after one look at her outraged face, "but they're not realistic. They—"

"But—"

"—build something with lots of panels and blinking lights that won't even lift off the ground," he continued ruthlessly, " and expect the audience to believe it's going to outer space."

"But it's just a story! You're supposed to pretend," she added with emphasis.

He poked at his chicken and speared the last bite. "They're going to have to build a believable product before I buy the story," he stated calmly.

I take it all back, Charlie, she mentally addressed the missing man. He's been in that lab too long.

Alerted by her silence, Brand looked up. "Well? What's the verdict? Am I hopeless?"

"Almost. But I'll give you one more chance. Tell me just one thing that makes you laugh. I don't mean just a smile, either. I mean a real belly laugh."

"My housekeeper and my dog," he answered promptly.

"Two? I don't believe it. Tell me about them," she demanded.

His lips curved in a sudden, wicked grin that surprised Dena so much she choked on the last bit of veal she had just popped into her mouth. Brand reached over, thumped her on the back and watched as she dabbed at her eyes.

"No, I won't spoil it. I want you to meet them."

"When?"

"Tomorrow morning? Will you come for breakfast?"

"If it can be brunch," she said, making a sudden decision, " its a deal."

His nod was decisive. "You're on. But why so late? Do you sleep in on Saturdays?"

"Nope. As a matter of fact, I'll be up before dawn and I'd like you to join me. Interested?"

"I suppose you're not going to tell me any more than that," he said in resignation.

"I'll tell you this much," she said kindly. "Dress warm and be ready for hard work."

Chapter Six

Is it okay to eat in here?''

At Brand's nod, Dena thrust two steaming mugs of coffee in his outstretched hands and slid into his car. She tore open a paper bag and placed four warm croissants between them.

They sat quietly, munching the rolls, savoring the heat of the coffee. Slowly, the windows fogged up, closing out the cold, dark morning, compressing their immediate world to the plush interior of the car.

Dena was wearing a down jacket, knit cap, and jeans. Not the designer type, he noted. They were clearly worn for work, not style. Even so, they faithfully clung to the flare of her derriere, and followed the intriguing curves from her thighs to her ankles. A warmth stirred low in his body, reminding him of the hours since he had last kissed her. Keeping one eye on his coffee, he shifted beneath the steering wheel, swearing softly to himself.

The last thing he needed right now was the distraction of a maddening, inconsistent, and provoking...enchantress. Automatically, he clarified his statement. He could do without the distraction, but not without her. And she was beginning to get the message.

He remembered the wary expression on her face when he took her home from the restaurant. All he could think about was that damn red dress and what was beneath it. He had not been subtle. He grinned in the darkness. She'd been more than a match for him.

"Thank you for standing in for John and for the delicious dinner," she had said, accepting the key from him and remaining in the doorway.

"You're not inviting me in?" he asked, his gaze drifting down from her determined chin to the shadowy invitation between her breasts.

Her voice was as calm as her gaze as it followed, and finally intercepted, his. "You look too hungry," she said in amusement. "I think not."

"It's been a long time since I kissed a woman good-night at the door."

She grinned. "Maybe we should take a rain check."

He reached for her. "And maybe we shouldn't." He drew her to him, pleased when her eyes widened and the pulse in her throat rose crazily. He wrapped his arms around her, muttering about the inordinate amount of material in the coat, while savoring the softness beneath it. And the red dress.

She was right, he discovered, kissing her. He was hungry. More than that, he decided. Starved—for her and her rare combination of strength and softness, cool intelligence and warm reactions. Warmth? he wondered as he slowly unbuttoned her coat and slipped his arms inside, closing them around her again. No, he had named it already. Fire.

When he finally raised his head, it was to watch with pleasure as her eyes opened slowly, hazy and content with sensuality. His heart jumped at the look on her face as he laced his hands through her honey-colored hair. He could, he realized with wonder, make this woman—his woman—simmer at his touch. Fiercely, but unwisely, he grinned.

Her eyes widened with an almost audible snap. They also cooled far more quickly than he would have believed possible. She wore her composure like another wrap.

"I've really got to go in now. Would you do something for me before you leave?"

He agreed, cursing his clumsiness.

Whipping off her coat, she turned her back to him. "Would you pull the zipper down for me? I love the dress," she said as he touched the back of her neck, "but it's hard to get on and impossible to get off."

He shifted again, remembering her revenge. He'd opened the damned zipper and she had whisked inside, reminding him to be early. Driving home, he recalled how his knuckle had brushed her bare flesh, all the way down her back. He'd gotten very little sleep.

"Ah, that's the only way to start the day," Dena said a few minutes later. Her eyes had lost their drowsy look, the croissants were gone, and the coffee level was low enough for safe driving.

While he was debating the wisdom of suggesting another, even more pleasurable way to greet the morning, she sat up and briskly declared, "Enough of this lollygagging, we've got places to go and things to do. I'll hold your coffee while you get this jet underway."

"Where to?" he asked, reluctantly turning the ignition key.

"Morgan Hill."

He looked at her questioningly.

"South of San Jose," she added.

"I know where it is. I just don't see why—"

"You'll find out. Now if you'll just get on the freeway and follow your nose, I'll close my eyes and grab another few minutes of sleep. Call out when we near the turnoff, and I'll direct you from there."

"Are you sure the weather's going to be warm enough for whatever we're doing? It's cold enough out here to freeze the—"

"Watch your language," she warned lazily. "The weatherman promised today would be a carbon copy of yesterday. That'll be plenty warm."

He drove in silence for about fifteen minutes before he said, "Morgan Hill coming up."

Dena allowed herself one last luxurious stretch. Straightening, she opened eyes bright with anticipation. Guiding him through town and down an inconspicuous road, she directed, "Park over here."

Brand killed the motor and looked around. "This is what you do for laughs?" he inquired. "So far, I've crawled out of bed in the middle of the night, frozen my butt off, not to mention my fingers and toes, to park on the edge of an empty field where all I can see is my breath."

"Don't kid me. You're having a ball and you know it. Actually," she admitted, "this hobby isn't one for a lot of laughs. Once the work is over, it's more along the line of quiet enjoyment. And as far as not being able to see anything, there'll be plenty of action in a little while. We just got here first. See?"

She pointed back the way they had come. Headlights were curving around the bend in the road. Within ten minutes, the sky slipped from black to gray and a small caravan of pickups, trailers and cars had trickled onto the field.

"Come on." She nudged Brand. "It's not much colder out there than it is in here. It'll soon be dawn. The magic time."

He looked around curiously. "Is this what I think it is?"

She gestured like a magician waving his wand and said simply, "Hot air balloons. These are the early birds. By the time the sun hits the horizon, some of them will have their balloons inflated and ready to go." She linked her arm through his. "Let's walk around. I think you'll be interested in this."

Some time later, Dena admitted that she may have just uttered the understatement of the year. The sun had warmed the bitter chill in the air, but Brand had forgotten his terminal case of frostbite.

He watched as three men wrestled a bulky, nylon box from a pickup to the ground.

"That weighs between five and six hundred pounds," Dena informed him. He nodded absently, absorbing the information, oblivious of its source. Fifteen minutes later, the enormous balloon was stretched out on the scrubby grass, resembling nothing more than a multi-colored ribbon.

"That one's as tall as an eight-story building," she commented.

"How do you know?"

"Because it's the same size as mine." A small smile curved her lips as she waited. It didn't take long.

His intent gaze, which had missed nothing so far, swiveled to her. "You own one?"

She nodded. "In partnership with a couple of friends. They'll be along soon. You'd better keep an eye on those guys because you'll be doing the same thing in a little while."

A large rotary fan was set up near the mouth of the balloon. "I'll be damned," he muttered. "As simple as that. It just blows the air in." When it was partially inflated, one of the men entered with a burner, and a flame about eight feet long shot out in front of him.

"The only trick to that," Dena said dryly, "is making sure the balloon's inflated enough so you don't burn the nylon. See over there?" she pointed to the side. "It's tied to the ground because, with the hot air in it, it'll soon be standing straight up."

All around them, balloons were ponderously rising to upright positions, tugging at their tethers.

Wicker gondolas, equipped with propane tanks and burners, were attached. Passengers were crawling or, depending upon their agility, being hauled into the high-sided baskets, waiting impatiently to be airborne.

Dena's gesture encompassed the entire field. "This is the time I love the most, when the sun is over the hill and you can see all the brilliant colors. Look! The first one is lifting off!"

Brand reluctantly tore his gaze from her radiant face and looked around. He could understand her enchantment. The air was clear and crisp, and the colors were dazzling. Most of the balloons had vertical stripes of pure, bright hues, but some had broad horizontal stripes. The colors were limited only by the imagination, he decided. One balloon looked like an enormous bouquet with green stems branching out from the base, topped with colorful creations that resembled poppies and daisies. Another was shaped like a beer bottle.

He reached out and drew Dena closer, urging her in front of him. Never taking his eyes off the colorful scene, he wrapped his arms around her and rested his chin on her head. One by one, the balloons drifted slowly upward until the sky resembled an Easter basket strewn with vividly hued eggs. The silence was broken only by the excited chatter of the passengers and the occasional hiss of a burner.

Dena's elbow in his ribs brought Brand back to the present. "Come on, it's our turn now." She steered him across the field where two husky young men were laying out a balloon. Bringing him to a halt, she said simply, "Brand, meet my partners and friends, Mike Penzer and Jack Horton. Guys, this is Brand McAllister.''

For a moment, the three men regarded each other, Dena thought with amusement, like three strange dogs intent on claiming a new territory. Finally, the taller of the two, a redhead, stepped forward with his hand extended. ''Hi, how ya doing?'' he asked casually. ''I'm Mike.''

The second one, broader and darker, followed suit. ''Jack,'' he said in a quiet voice. ''You're a surprise,'' he continued. ''Shortstuff—'' he put a hand on Dena's shoulder ''—doesn't usually bring anyone out here.'' Without seeming to move, they fell in beside Dena, making it a three-to-one split as they faced Brand.

With eyes full of speculation, he considered the two men. They had made a definite statement and were now awaiting an answer. He took his time, sliding his hands into the back pockets of his jeans. Dena, he noted, had opted out of the action. His attention was back on the two men. Young, protective, but without the perception to judge whether or not she needed two burly guardians. Good material, but not up to his weight or experience.

His voice was crisp, subtly pulling rank. ''If this is an example of your protective methods for Dena, you've obviously been doing a good job. I appreciate it. But—'' he leaned forward, swiftly plucked her from between the two and tucked her under his arm ''—you can safely leave her in my hands now. I'll take good care of her.'' He stood there, relaxed and waiting.

The two looked at Dena, at each other, then back at Brand. Grinning, Jack asked, "Well, are we going to get this thing up today or not?"

Half-an-hour later, Brand and Dena were standing in the gondola. There had been a momentary confusion when Dena handed him what looked like a motorcycle helmet. "Protects your head from the heat of the burner," she explained. It was then he understood that she was the pilot. "Any comments?" She arched a questioning brow.

"How long have you had your license?"

"Two years." She examined his resigned expression, nodded briefly, and leaned over the side. "Let her go, guys."

They rose silently, so gently that only the creak of the wicker and the whoosh of the burner testified to the motion. There was no sense of movement, no rushing force of air ruffling their hair. They moved with the wind, much as a leaf would drift with the current.

Brand examined the burner. "Hard to believe this can heat all that air," he muttered, looking straight up into the balloon.

Dena tapped his shoulder with a determined finger. "I didn't get up in the middle of the night and drag you here so you could inspect a machine. You can play with that when we're through. For now, would you please look down at the countryside? It's lovely at this time of the year."

Propping her elbows on the padded suede rim, she sighed with pleasure. "Look at that. It reminds me of New England in the fall." They drifted toward green rolling hills which in turn led to the oak woodlands of the Diablo Mountain Range. The

Take 4 Books
–and a Mystery Gift–
FREE

**And preview exciting new Silhouette Romance novels
every month—as soon as they're published!**

Silhouette Romance®

Yes...Get 4 Silhouette Romance novels (a $7.80 value) along with your Mystery Gift FREE

SLIP AWAY FOR AWHILE... Let Silhouette Romance draw you into a love-filled world of fascinating men and women. You'll find it's easy to close the door on the cares and concerns of everyday life as you lose yourself in the timeless drama of love, played out in exotic locations the world over.

EVERY BOOK AN ORIGINAL... Every Silhouette Romance is a full-length story, never before in print, superbly written to give you more of what you want from romance. Start with 4 brand new Silhouette Romance novels—yours free with the attached coupon. Along with your Mystery Gift, it's a $7.80 gift from us to you, with no obligation to buy anything now or ever.

YOUR FAVORITE AUTHORS... Sihouette Romance novels are created by the very best authors of romantic fiction. Let your favorite authors—such as Brittany Young, Diana Palmer, Janet Dailey, Nora Roberts, and many more—take you to a whole other world.

ROMANCE-FILLED READING... Each month you'll meet lively young heroines and share in their trials and triumphs...bold, virile men you'll find as fascinating as the heroines do...and colorful supporting characters you'll feel you've known forever. They're all in Silhouette Romance novels—and now you can share every one of the wonderful reading adventures they provide.

NO OBLIGATION... Each month we'll send you 6 brand-new Silhouette Romance novels. Your books will be sent to you as soon as they are published, without obligation. If not enchanted, simply return them within 15 days and owe nothing. Or keep them, and pay just $1.95 each (a total of $11.70). And there's never an additional charge for shipping and handling.

SPECIAL EXTRAS FOR HOME SUBSCRIBERS ONLY... When you take advantage of this offer and become a home subscriber, we'll also send you the Silhouette Books Newsletter FREE with each book shipment. Every informative issue features news about upcoming titles, interviews with your favorite authors, even their favorite recipes.

So send in the postage-paid card today, and take your fantasies further than they've ever been. The trip will do you good!

CLIP AND MAIL COUPON TODAY!

NO POSTAGE
NECESSARY
IF MAILED
IN THE
UNITED STATES

BUSINESS REPLY CARD

FIRST CLASS   PERMIT NO. 194   CLIFTON, N.J.

Postage will be paid by addressee

Silhouette Books
120 Brighton Road
P.O. BOX 5084
Clifton, NJ 07015-9956

leafy trees ranged from deep green to gold and scarlet in celebration of the cooler season.

Brand leaned forward, placing a hand on either side of Dena. Her contented survey of the land below ended abruptly as she became aware of the warmth radiating from his body. "'Scuse me," she muttered, ducking under his arm to reach the burner. She needed her wits about her while piloting the balloon. That had never before been a problem but then she had never been enclosed in the small gondola with someone like Brand McAllister.

"Why did you take off after almost everyone else had gone?" he asked.

"Several reasons. Most of the others take paying passengers and plan to make at least two trips, which means they need an earlier start. We don't do that. A big part of my pleasure comes from watching all the others. Mike and Jack understand that, and fortunately they're bigger on working than looking. They tell me that I'm not a heck of a lot of help, anyway," she said with a grin.

"Doesn't that bother you?"

"Uh-uh. I may not have big muscles, but when they're up here, they need me down there." Brand's gaze followed her pointing finger to the fields below.

"How so?"

"While we're up here, they become the searcher crew. When they're up, I'm it." They had been drifting downward, so she turned the burner on and waited until they rose several hundred feet. "Did you think we circled around and landed back in the field?"

He shrugged. "Hadn't thought about it at all."

"We never know which way the breeze will take us, so someone below always follows." She leaned forward and pointed. "Mike and Jack are in the blue pickup over there. It's my responsibility to land in a decent place, and it's theirs to be waiting. Then we either switch places or fold up the balloon and go home."

The rest of the flight was made in companionable silence broken only by an occasional comment. Dena made frequent checks of the altimeter and pressure gauges. Once she pointed down to a horse grazing in a field. It jerked to attention, looked around and broke into a nervous trot. "Our shadow caused that reaction," she said in a low voice.

They landed in a field covered with scrub grass where Mike and Jack were waiting to steady the gondola. The four of them deflated the balloon and had it back in the truck within thirty minutes. Dena reached into the cooler and pulled out a bottle of champagne and some plastic stemware.

"This is to celebrate your first flight," she informed Brand as she and the two men raised their glasses in his direction.

"First?"

"You're either hooked on the first one or you're not. I think you'll go up again." When they were done, she packed away the bottle and glasses and climbed into the back of the truck with the balloon. Gesturing for Brand to join her, she turned to Mike and Jack. "Okay, slaves. You can take us back to the field now."

Saluting with mock respect, they turned to the truck.

"Why didn't they go up? Don't they mind coming out just for us?" Brand drew Dena closer and held her securely as the truck bumped over the rutted dirt road.

"They didn't want to, and no," she answered precisely. "I come out a lot when they want to take someone up. Today was just for you," she added quietly.

Her statement called for no particular answer, but she was still surprised when she received none. Eventually, he broke the silence.

"Jack said you don't often take people up."

"That's right."

His silvery gaze rested on her serene face. A face that was giving nothing away. He couldn't tell if she arranged the flight as a mere whim, a test of some sort, or an impulsive decision to share something that was important to her. He hoped it was the latter. It *had* to be. He wanted to fill her thoughts, to take over her waking and sleeping moments, the way she was tormenting his. In a quiet voice he finally said, "Thank you. I think you shared something with me that's very special to you." He lowered his head and kissed her softly on the cheek. They rode back to the field in thoughtful silence.

Minutes later, they were in the Porsche heading north.

"Hungry?"

The car was warm, the music soft, and for once Brand seemed to have turned off his potent sensuality. Dena was lost in the soft-cushioned seat, content to be swept along in the powerful car. She lazily opened an eye but before she could say anything her stomach gurgled noisily. "Would you believe me if I said no?"

"Not now. Hang on for another ten minutes or so and you'll be sitting down to the best brunch in Silicon Valley."

"That good, huh?"

"The best. Maybe the country club could outdo it, but I wouldn't bet on it."

"Where'd you find this treasure?"

"Inherited is more like it."

She sat up straight, eyes bright with curiosity. "You don't inherit people."

"I don't know what else to call it."

"Explain, please."

"Several years ago, Charlie rescued this cook from an awkward situation in a foreign country. He decided that nothing was too good for him—"

"Wait a minute. Charlie?"

"No, the cook. Out of gratitude, he said he would take over—"

"He? The cook?"

"—The running of Charlie's household and simplify his life."

"Charlie's?"

"Of course, isn't that what I said?"

They had reached the outskirts of Cupertino and were winding up one of the hillside roads. While she was trying to figure out exactly what he *had* said, Brand pulled into a long driveway and parked before a sprawling ranch-style house.

Before they reached the door, it was thrown open. Dena skidded to a stop and stood gawking. A very large man with a shock of white hair and eyes the color of pea soup filled the opening. He had hands the size of hams and a white towel was tucked in the waist of his jeans. His brawny arms were covered with tattoos that she would give a month's salary to inspect. If Charlie had rescued this one, she thought, it hadn't been from a monastery. In fact, it boggled her mind to think of him needing rescuing at all. He looked like he belonged on the high seas, swinging from a rope with a knife between his teeth.

"You're late," he bit out. "The soufflé fell." Turning, he stomped away, the rattling of vases and glassware accompanying each step.

"Is that—" She bit back a smile, unable to complete her question.

He nodded. "My housekeeper."

"But, how—"

"Did I end up with him?"

She nodded.

He ushered her in and closed the door. "Charlie. He told Nick that he already had someone taking care of him. God only knows what else he told him, but somehow I became the recipient of his gratitude."

"Didn't Charlie clear it with you?"

"He said he did," he answered, leading her down a hall.

"Obviously, you agreed."

"He said I did."

"Wait a minute." She tugged at his shirt and pulled him to a halt. "Don't you remember?"

He ran a hand through his hair. "Actually, no. I was doing some pretty heavy research at the time and wasn't paying much attention to what Charlie said. First thing I knew about it was when I came home late one night. I was putting the key in the lock and Nick jerked open the door. Scared the hell out of me. I thought I had a burglar on my hands. A big one.''

Dena leaned against him, giggling. ''Then what?''

''He told me his name, that Charlie had sent him, and that he had moved in during the day.'' His expression was rueful. ''That was three years ago.'' He gestured toward a door. ''If you want to wash up, the bathroom's in there.''

Five minutes later she emerged and followed her nose to the dining room.

''Are you expecting an army?'' Brand was asking the older man as she entered the room. He was obviously referring to the quantities of food spread all over the table and a sideboard.

''Your note said that you were bringing friends home for brunch.''

''Friend. One. Singular.''

The older man scowled. ''If you'd learn to write, it might help.'' He pulled a paper out of his back pocket. ''Just look at this hen scratching. If this doesn't say 'friends,' I'll eat it, bad writing and all. I'll bet if she read it—'' he tilted his head at Dena ''—she'd say the same thing.''

Unable to believe her luck, Dena held out her hand. Could it be this simple, she wondered. Was she about to be rewarded for her patience and restraint? She had nobly refrained from using any devious methods to obtain some of his papers from work. Now, hardly believing that she was going to see more of his writing than his initials, she reached for the note—only to have Brand intercept it just as her fingertips brushed the paper. He folded it and stuffed it in his shirt pocket, smiling sardonically at her sigh of frustration.

"Nick, this is Dena Trevor." He held a chair for her as he spoke. "She isn't big enough to make a dent in all this food. I think you'd better join us."

Nick measured her with his eyes and seemed to agree. He turned and stomped through the swinging door into the kitchen.

"Is he mad?"

"No. He always walks that way. A Nureyev he's not. I've learned to tie things down that I don't want broken."

Nick returned almost on the next swing of the door. He had whipped the towel from around his waist and was eyeing the food hungrily. "I was running late this morning and didn't stop to eat," he said, pulling up a chair across from Dena. "So where have you two been, and why are you late?"

"Hot-air ballooning," Brand mumbled, wolfing down a blueberry muffin.

"No kidding? I've always wanted to go up in one of those things."

"If you'll give me the recipe for these muffins," Dena said, "I'll take you up on a flight."

Nick turned to Brand in surprise. "She the pilot?" he asked, cocking a thick thumb in her direction.

Brand nodded.

Dena watched a series of expressions run across the square face that had been scored and furrowed by life. He was obviously a man's man. It had not surprised him when she requested a recipe, but he wasn't so sure she could control a balloon.

Dena was amused and it showed in her voice. "She's the pilot. She also has excellent hearing and can speak for herself."

"You one of them women-libbers?" he asked cautiously.

"Do you feel that your masculinity is on the line because you wear a towel as an apron and work in a kitchen?" she countered.

He snorted. "Hell, I don't have to prove anything. I know what I am."

"Exactly." She almost crowed in triumph. "So do I." She swallowed a bite of the most delicious egg concoction she had ever tasted. "Do I get my recipe?"

He looked at her thoughtfully, then nodded. "For free." He picked up a glazed cinnamon roll and eyed it approvingly. "No obligation."

He had the look of a man who was backpedaling as fast as he could, Dena decided. She had the feeling that he rarely shared his recipes. But he'd probably hand over his entire collection with a smile if that meant he didn't have to deliver his hulking frame into her care.

"In that case, I guess I'll have to refuse," she sighed, with an almost imperceptible lift at the corner of her mouth. "But, if you ever decide you want that ride, I'll be delighted to accept the recipe." She lowered her lashes, blotting out the sight of his startled expression. It'd be a shame to ruin her wistful performance by giggling.

Nick got up, poured coffee in their cups and sat down again muttering beneath his breath about stubborn women. Turning his muddy-green eyes on Brand, he demanded, "You got that problem at work taken care of?"

Brand popped a piece of bacon in his mouth and gestured at Dena. "There's my white witch. She's coming to work Monday to help me wrap the whole thing up."

Nick looked dubious. "She's awful small."

Enough was enough, Dena decided. "But she's smart," she stated with asperity. "And believe it or not, the last time she checked, intelligence wasn't being measured by the size of a person's biceps."

He regarded her enigmatically, then turned to Brand. "Feisty little thing, isn't she?" he drawled.

Chapter Seven

Brand choked on his coffee.

Dena alleviated her exasperation by whacking him on the back. When peace was restored, she placed her napkin on the table and thanked them both for the delicious meal. She pointedly avoided commenting on the company.

"I thought you said you had a dog." A rather abrupt change of subject, she allowed, but then her present company seemed to favor direct speaking over the subtle approach. When in Rome, she decided grimly, emulate the natives.

Brand wiped his eyes on his napkin and turned to Nick. "Have you seen him?"

Nick glumly eyed all the food left on the table before he answered. "In his usual place. We're going to be eating this stuff for the rest of the week, you know."

"I'll run Dena up and down the hill to work up an appetite and make her stay to dinner. You can heat up some of the things we didn't get around to trying."

There speaks a man who has never in his life been concerned with serving a balanced meal, and who doesn't care what he puts into his stomach as long as it's sufficient to quell the hunger pangs, Dena thought with amusement. Nick was regarding him with open disgust. Muttering something that sounded like 'Arggh,' he swept up an armload of dishes and thundered into the kitchen.

"Come on," Brand said, leading her down the hall and into a large, comfortable room whose walls consisted either of books or windows. A large golden retriever lay asleep on the creamy carpet in front of the fireplace. Sunlight shafted through the windows, enhancing the golden highlights of his coat, which gleamed like a new copper penny.

Dena walked closer, admiring the magnificently sprawled animal. "What a beauty." At that, the dog opened one weary eye, groaned deeply, and obviously exhausted by the effort, closed it again.

Brand joined her, nodding. Affectionate disgust played over his face. "He's also the laziest, dumbest dog I've ever seen."

"What's his name?"

"Red."

"How original."

"He is red," Brand pointed out.

"Undeniably. Using that logic, you could have also called him 'Dog.'"

Grinning, Brand said, "I thought of that, but I liked Red better."

Dena nudged the inanimate dog with the toe of her shoe. The only reaction was another groan. She called his name. A muscle quivered in one long ear.

She glanced up at Brand, noting that he wasn't surprised. "I give up. How do you get him to budge?"

Moving to a sliding glass door, he advised, "Move back. You're in the direct line of fire."

At the click of the handle, Red sprang to startled attention. Two mad leaps later, he was flying out the door.

"What on earth's out there?"

Brand gestured for her to precede him, closing the door behind them. "Come on. You won't want to miss this."

Hand in hand, they ran after the galloping animal. Rounding the corner of the house, they watched as Red approached the patio's tile decking at a dead run and leaped into the deep end of the swimming pool. He swam to the shallow end and climbed up the stairs just as they arrived. His shining coat, now a deep auburn, clung to his muscular body. Leaving an erratic trail of water behind him, Red pranced over to join them.

From long experience, Brand backed away. Dena's laughter at the blissful expression on the dog's face broke off as he came nearer.

"Dog," she threatened, retreating until she fell backward into a deck chair, "don't you dare. Shoo! Go away!" Trapped by the cavorting animal, she lifted her feet to the edge of the chair, pressed her face to her knees and waited for the deluge. "Brand," she wailed as a spray of cold water hit her, "make him go away!"

Cautiously lifting her head, she glared at the man laughing down at her. "Big help you are." Before he could answer, Red reared up, propped his huge paws on her shoulders and swiped the side of her face with a big, pink tongue. His weight toppled her until she was pinned to the back of the redwood chair and she let out a yelp as the other side of her face was bathed by the drippy tongue.

"Enough is enough," she declared, planting the soles of her shoes against his chest and gently pushing. Red dropped to his feet, dashed off to diligently search the area, found what he was looking for and loped back to Dena.

Waving her arms like a windmill, she cried, "No! I don't want—"

Bouncing with excess energy, his plumed tail making sweeping arcs, Red sashayed over and laid a large, muddy branch across her legs.

"—that dirty thing in my lap." She eyed the stick with resignation, and glared first at the dancing dog, then up at its owner.

"That was a double seal of approval," Brand commented. "He doesn't kiss everyone, and he's very selective when it comes to picking a partner to play with."

Her voice was dry as she observed the lolling tongue and bright eyes. "Funny. I wouldn't have thought discrimination was one of his finer qualities." Rising, she said with a sigh, "I guess I'm supposed to throw this for him."

"You'll be his friend for life," Brand assured her. "Although mud puddles are his top priority, and he'll drop anything to wallow in one, playing catch runs a close second. Once you throw things for him, he never forgets. He could find you in the middle of Times Square on New Year's Eve."

"Terrific." She brushed clumps of caked dirt off the stick, gingerly grasped it by one end and heaved it as far as she could. Watching Red gallop down the yard, she brushed her hands on the seat of her jeans and declared, "I draw the line at mud puddles. I gave them up when I was five."

Less than an hour later, she was eating her words. Red rarely returned with the same object thrown, so Dena had handled a variety of sticks, balls and Frisbees. Not one of them, she decided, examining her mud-spattered clothes, had been even semi-clean. To be fair, it wasn't all his fault. No one had forced her to engage him in a tug-of-war when he refused to surrender a nicely balanced throwing stick. How was she to know that he would cheat by backing her into a boggy flower bed, pulling her off balance and then letting go of the stick?

Brand called time, pushing a besotted dog away from Dena. He examined the two of them and decided that there wasn't a whit of difference between their degrees of dirtiness.

He took the nozzle off the hose and turned the full force of the water on Red, cleaning him. Turning to Dena, he said, "I think you ought to come in the house and clean up."

"Oh, God no, anything but that. Tommy Tattoo will take one look at me and call the sanitation department. Can't you just take me home?"

"Not yet. You're wearing half my garden and I'd prefer that you got rid of it before you get in the car."

Dena's prediction was close to the truth. When she walked in the service porch, Nick looked up.

"Jeez, will you look at that? What'd she do? Fall in every mud puddle on the block? Give her something to wear, and I'll throw her clothes in the washer."

Dena closed her eyes, prayed for an extra measure of patience, and followed Brand.

The following Monday morning at the stroke of eight, Dena entered John's office. Looking at the rangy, dark man, she wondered again at the curious chemistry that existed between the sexes. What was it that allowed her to regard such a handsome and thoroughly nice man as a substitute brother, while her pulse accelerated at an alarming rate whenever she encountered a certain complex man, a supreme pragmatist whose thinking took the form of empirical logic?

A smile warmed Dena's face as she dropped down in a chair. Facing him across the width of his desk, she said, "Hi, boss. Where do you want me and how are we organizing this thing?"

John leaned back, lacing his fingers behind his head, openly studying the woman before him. She was wearing a teal-blue dress with full sleeves cuffed and buttoned at the wrist. The neckline was low enough to be interesting and high enough to be considered businesslike. The effect was one of a woman comfortable with her sexuality and certain of her competency.

His voice was dry when he got around to answering her. "Speaking of bosses, ours wasn't happy when he found out that we had a date. How long have you two—"

"We haven't been," she interrupted. "Well, I suppose we have, but not long...and not seriously. Or exclusively."

He grimaced. "I don't want to see him any more serious than he was Friday afternoon."

"What do you mean?"

"He gave me enough work to keep me busy for a week and asked if I could have it on his desk before I left that night."

"But what makes you think that it had anything to do with me?"

"Come on, Dena. Brand isn't known for his subtlety, but he normally doesn't come down like a sledgehammer. And that's exactly what he did. He let me know that, as far as he was concerned, he was serious. And feeling very exclusive. Even possessive."

She grinned. "You don't say."

"I do say."

She was thoughtful, her eyes full of speculation. He *had* been acting a bit territorial. Like the time he had plucked her from between Mike and Jack and informed them that he would take care of her. Yes, you could call that possessive. She was surprised at how much pleasure the thought gave her. Deciding that she would think about it later when she could devote more time to all of the ramifications, she asked again, "Where do you want me to work?"

He got up and held the door open. As they walked down the hall, he said, "I had a small office set up for you. I know you don't need much except the basics, so it's just a desk, telephone, and a couple of chairs."

"That's fine," she murmured absently, as they stopped at an open door branching off the main office. "Is this it?"

"Uh-huh." His gesture included the four walls and the sparse furnishings. "Will it do?"

She nodded, walked in and sat at the desk. The room was small, but more than adequate. Best of all, it was close to the bank of personnel files.

John perched on the corner of the desk. "I had a printout run of everyone who has worked in the lab or had any reason to be there, and someone started pulling their files first thing this morning. The first batch should be arriving soon. How long do you thing it'll take you?"

"About how many are there?"

"A lot. We're pulling everyone from the engineers to the clerical staff and custodians." One dark brow rose, tacitly repeating his question.

"Each file will go fast, maybe fifteen to thirty seconds. All I have to do is open it and find a sample of the person's writing. I'll know right away. It's a bit like looking for a familiar face in a crowd. It's either there or it's not." She paused, looking up. "Does that answer your question?"

"Yeah." He frowned down at his black leather shoes. "I guess."

Puzzled by his reaction, she asked, "How's your printout organized. Alphabetically?"

"No. Usually in a situation like this, the culprit turns out to be someone who understands the material, someone working directly on the scene. So I've arranged it to start with the engineers and others in the lab and then on to the peripheral workers.''

"So what's the problem?"

He sighed and prowled the office restlessly. "It's one thing to read about high-tech crime, it's another to be in the middle of it. You're getting the files of all the people who have a reason to be in that area. But what if that note came from someone who *doesn't* belong there? Someone who got in there on some flimsy pretext? You might have to check out everyone in the entire company. It could take several weeks."

Dena remembered the closed circuit television monitors and all the steps taken by Protective Services. It didn't seem likely that there was any slack in the security, she thought. But not knowing if John was familiar with the control room, she said nothing. At the same time, she made a mental note to ask Brand. She had promised to say nothing of what she had seen, but if she and John were to collaborate on this project, they should be able to discuss all aspects of it.

"By the way," she asked, "what have your people been told about me?"

He grinned. "Your fictitious foundation is alive and well. My staff thinks that you're doing research. And, as long as you don't make more work for the rest of them, they really don't care."

If he had planned to say more on the subject, he was interrupted by a brief knock on the open door. "This where you want these files?" A head covered with short brown curls followed the voice. It apparently decided that this was indeed the place, and withdrew. Two black rubber wheels attached to a dolly that carried three boxes of files rolled through the door. Behind it was a tall angular woman with a placid expression.

"This is the first batch. Will you want the others today?" At Dena's nod, she stood the dolly upright, slid it from beneath the boxes and turned to leave. "In case you need me before I get back, my name's Millie." With that, she hustled through the door.

Dena's startled gaze followed her, then turned to John. "If everyone around here is that efficient, I'll be through before lunch. I'd better hop to it or she'll be back before I even get started."

She linked her arm through his and turned to the door, just in time to see a familiar face. Jerking to a halt, she whispered, "John, who's the escapee from muscle beach out there? The Blond Bombshell with the mustache and profile?"

At his look of incomprehension, Dena pointed toward a desk in the corner of the room. "I met him the other day, along with four other people, and I can't remember his name. He's either Mr. Silver or—"

"Wayne Randall. You've just restored my faith in women. Every female in this office falls apart when he walks in. It takes at least ten minutes for them to remember how to answer a telephone once he leaves."

"And they say that women exaggerate." But she took another peek to see if she had missed anything beyond the obvious good looks.

"Scout's honor." John raised his right hand.

"I probably have bad taste," she said, "but I've never been partial to blonds. Is he conceited?"

"I don't think so. He's not a bad guy. But if you talk to him for more than two minutes, you'll hear about his new car. The company just presented him with a new Porsche for some fancy brainwork. He solved a problem that had been holding up one of our projects."

"That's some bonus check," Dena said dryly.

"Good economics," he replied succinctly. "He saved the company a bundle and that's how they showed their appreciation." Checking his watch, he said, "I've got to go. Good luck. Call me if you need anything."

Dena dug a couple of pencils out of the top drawer and lifted the first box to her desk. After easing the folders out right side up, she put the box on the floor so she could replace the files in their original order. She didn't know if it would help Millie when refiling them, but she would do what she could to relieve the woman's tedious task.

Opening the first folder, she flipped through the papers until she found something written by the employee. One quick glance was sufficient. She closed the file and put it in the box. Wishing that they were all recent employees, she reached for the second one. When Charlie hired her, she'd persuaded him to revamp the application form to include a half-page space for a written statement by the applicant. Smiling in satisfaction, she flipped to the revised form in the second file. Her smile faded as she looked at the large, round writing. It was nothing at all like the note. The second folder joined the first.

Three more had been added to the box when a woman appeared in the doorway. She introduced herself as Linda and announced that it was time for a coffee break. Dena got up, murmured her own name, and reluctantly followed her guide.

Twenty minutes later, Dena settled back behind the desk. She had just picked up the next file when someone tapped on the door. Sighing, she dropped the folder, leaned back in her chair and looked up to meet the interested gaze of Wayne Randall.

He stepped in and perched on the arm of the other chair. "Hi. I saw you working and just wanted to say hello. Am I interrupting anything?"

"Not a thing," she said, wishing it weren't the truth. Dena wondered how the man ever managed to solve enough complex problems to be given a car. As far as she could tell, he had spent the morning in Personnel instead of in the lab. Of course, she didn't really care where he holed up as long as it wasn't in her office.

"I hear congratulations are in order," she commented when it seemed that he had nothing further to say. At the look of inquiry in his blue eyes, she said, "Your car. I understand that you were just given a new one."

A flash of enthusiasm crossed his face. "It's really a honey. Say, what are you doing at lunchtime?"

Blinking at the sudden non sequitur, she said, "Eating, I suppose."

"No." He shifted impatiently. "I mean before, or after. Would you like to walk out to the lot and see the car?"

Dena tried to muster up a look of enthusiasm. She was, she understood, being offered a rare treat. She was also totally uninterested. In her opinion, cars were simply a means of transportation. As long as they took her from one point to another without dying on the way, they fulfilled her requirements. The only thing she could comment knowledgeably about was their color, and she had learned years ago that most men considered that worse than no comment at all. She'd also learned to conceal the fact that when buying a car, a radio, heater and air conditioner headed her priorities.

"I'd love it," she said, smiling weakly. "I've never known anyone who's been given a brand new car. Especially one like that."

"I earned it," he said. "As far as I'm concerned, it's all part of the package, like stock options or any other bonus."

"Are all companies this generous?" she asked curiously.

"No." He smoothed down his mustache. "This one ranks right at the top. That's why I'm here." He looked at the stack of folders on her desk. "It looks like you're off to a good start. Are you going through every file in the place?"

"Heavens no. I'd be here forever if I did that." She wished suddenly that she'd given more thought to her cover story.

"How did you pick the ones that you're checking?" he asked with casual interest.

Engineers, she thought in disgust. They need answers for everything. Now what could she tell him? Remembering bits and pieces from a computer class she had taken, she said slowly, "We devised a query listing ages, high stress jobs, and several other parameters. We fed it to the computer and, *voilà*, this is what we got."

"Hmm. Interesting. Is it done alphabetically?"

"I doubt it. Probably by job classification. I don't even look at the names," she told him, thinking that at least that much was true. "It's the information I'm after. It's eventually broken down and becomes statistics. So the names aren't important."

"Interesting," he said again, smothering a yawn and changing the subject. Twenty minutes later, he got up and stood before her desk. "Don't forget, I'll come by to show you the car."

"Terrific," she muttered, turning back to the folders before he was even through the door. She sifted through five of them before the telephone rang.

"Dena?" The deep voice was unmistakable. "I'll be down in a few minutes."

"What for?" she mumbled, tucking the phone between her shoulder and chin so she could reach for another file.

"Lunch."

"Lunch?" Didn't anyone work in this place? She dropped the folder and grabbed the receiver before it slid from its resting place. "Thanks anyway, but it's too early for me. I just got back from a coffee break. Besides, you're too late. I have a date with a car."

"Did you say—"

"Um-hmm, a car. I heard about Wayne Randall's new toy, was foolish enough to congratulate him, and now I get to spend my lunch hour in the parking lot staring at it."

"Serves you right," he said with callous amusement. "Okay, see you tonight for dinner. By the way, say whatever you want to about Randall's car, but don't touch it.''

Don't touch it? How could she look and not touch? And why should she? Mentally shrugging, she asked, "You don't happen to have a suggestion box around, do you?''

"Why?'' he asked lazily. "Do you have a complaint already?''

"On the contrary. I'm about to save you a great deal of money and earn *myself* a new car.'' Sternly controlling a quiver of laughter, she continued. "You see, so far this morning I've had a visitor, been taken for a coffee break, had another visitor, and am now told that lunch is right around the corner. So I had this terrific idea. It's called 'work.' You could save millions if you taught everyone how to slip a little of it in between breaks and—''

She looked at the receiver, which was now purring a dial tone at her. Smiling, she replaced it, reached for a file and almost dumped its contents on the desk when the bell pealed again.

Reaching for it, she heard Brand's voice say, "Shut your door, it works wonders.'' Once again, she heard the dial tone.

An hour later, she was saying, "It's gorgeous.'' She had been saying that, interspersed with "beautiful'' and "marvelous,'' for fifteen minutes and was rapidly running out of adjectives. Wayne had escorted her out to the farthest corner of the parking lot where there were fewer cars and less chance, he assured her, of the car being nicked and dented. He'd whipped off a light canvas cover and displayed the car as if he were revealing the crown jewels.

It was silvery-gray and Dena found herself comparing it to Brand's eyes. Almost the same shade, but it didn't have the glint of— Idiot! Of course, it didn't. It was only a car, while he was...a puzzle, to say the least. Oh well, onward. Think of something else to say about this marvelous, beautiful, glorious piece of tin on four wheels.

She reached out to touch the fender, and stopped. She had already made that mistake. Ignoring Brand's advice, she had leaned against the car. Several minutes passed before she became aware that Wayne's gaze repeatedly strayed to her hand resting on the hood. She moved away, pretending to be fascinated with some gadget on the dash and watched with resignation as he took out a white handkerchief and removed her fingerprints.

Now, while she watched, he replaced the cover, patted it in place, and tucked the car to bed. Looking up, he asked, "Ready to go back?"

Nodding, she turned and lengthened her stride to match his. "I just can't believe that companies do this very often."

His silence was thoughtful. "Stars are rewarded," he said finally. "Generously. At the moment, I happen to be one."

Dena darted a glance at his profile and wondered what was going on behind it. He was a quiet man for all his pride in the car, and didn't give much of himself away. Silicon Valley, she reminded herself, had given birth to a new breed of men. Their supreme intelligence was directed to incredibly fascinating projects—too fascinating. The lure of challenge occupied their attention twenty-four hours a day, seven days a week. For some, it replaced relationships, wives, and families.

"How did you happen to come to Mitchell's?"

He shrugged. "I had knowledge that was needed. I went to the highest bidder."

"That sounds awfully cold-blooded."

"Not really. Anyone looking for a job does the same thing. He adds up the pros and cons and opts for the most advantages. The only difference is that in the Valley, the bids are higher."

"What if someone offered you more now that you're settled here?"

"I'd probably go. Unless I was involved in something too interesting to leave. And Mitchell's understands that." He looked down at her, fingering his mustache, adding dryly, "That's why they give away Porsches. Too bad they're not as generous with reserved parking slots. I asked for one so the car wouldn't get all nicked up."

"What happened?"

He grimaced. "I got put in my place. They told me that only the top executives rated them."

Dena giggled. "Next time you do something clever, hold out for a parking spot."

That afternoon, behind the closed door, Dena finished the second box of files.

Chapter Eight

"Charlie? How are you?"

Brand leaned back on the sofa, watching Dena as she answered the telephone. His eyes skimmed over the silky dark green dress, tracing the line of her breasts, the hollow beneath her rib cage, the smooth flow of her hips and thighs. His fingers drifted over the delicate floral pattern on the brocade cushion next to his, unconsciously lingering on the section warmed by her body.

"Where are you now? The what? Andaman Islands? Where on earth—the *Bay of Bengal*?"

At the amused questions, his eyes lifted. The expressions chasing across her face were a blend of humor, concern, intelligence, curiosity—words failed him as he watched her. His lids lowered, masking the silvery eyes, allowing him to feast on the sight of her—the curves, the hollows, the femininity, the woman-to-his-man of her.

Thirty-four years. It had taken him that long to find her. Thirty-four years of not knowing that he was even searching. Years of believing that work was the panacea, the answer to everything. Well, now he knew. Knew that his future was unalterably bound with this woman, this contradictory bundle of strength and vulnerability. Now all he had to do was convince her.

"Wait a minute, Charlie. You tried to go ashore and they what?" Dena asked, stunned.

It shouldn't be that hard, Brand brooded. Once you know your goal, you block out your course of action. The large blocks are broken into smaller ones until the plan becomes workable. All you need is patience and persistence. His gaze rested moodily on her rounded bottom. And a hell of a lot of luck. Patience was the key word, he decided. You don't rush a woman like this. Especially not one who admitted, reluctantly, that she wasn't now nor had she ever— *"Arrows?* They *shot* at you? Are you all right?" Dena's agitation brought Brand back from his contemplation of the future. In one lithe move he was on his feet and by her side. Handing him the receiver, she said, "Here. You talk to the idiot."

Dena dropped down on the sofa and watched a frown gather on Brand's forehead. He'd had a rough day, and Charlie playing cowboys and Indians with the local natives wasn't helping. His conference with Security had been a repeat of the last one—lots of questions and no answers. And his white witch had failed. She'd been so sure about being able to match the writing, but her report had been negative. One big zip.

"Damn it, Charlie. You're supposed to be out there recuperating, not agitating the natives until they use you for a dartboard." Brand's exasperation crackled through the room. He ran his fingers through his thick hair as he listened. No, Dena's smile was barely more than a slight lift at the corners of her mouth, Brand wasn't really listening, he was waiting for Charlie to take a breath so he could finish his lecture.

Her gaze dropped from the breadth of his shoulders past the slim hips to long, strong legs. He hadn't gone home to change after work, and his charcoal jacket and gray slacks just enhanced his look of strength. His clothes were conservative and classical. They made a statement about the man, she decided, but not a total one. It would be a hard thing to do, she thought, because he's too much like...an iceberg. Not cold, she hastily assured herself. God knows he's far from that! Just more beneath the surface than above. A quiet man, a thinking man.

"Maybe they *like* wearing loin cloths. Have you thought of that?"

What would it be like living with such a man? she wondered. Difficult, to put it mildly. She had observed the change in him when they toured the labs. He touched metal and plastic as if it came alive beneath his hands. His words were practically lyrical as he explained the function of various pieces of equipment. He was utterly and completely fascinated with his work. How could a woman compete with that? Judging from the divorce rate in the area, most of them couldn't.

No, she thought slowly, regretfully, it would be no life for her. She had waited almost twenty-seven years to find a man who would be her other half. A man who would be a partner, a lover. She had a world of passion and love to share with that man. Share...that seemed to be the operative word. She was a giver by nature, but even givers need to be on the receiving end sometime. And she had the feeling she would be lost in a relationship with Brand.

He wasn't selfish or superficial, far from it. In the short week that she had known him, he'd exasperated her beyond measure and staggered her with his touch, his sensuality and, when she had his full attention, his understanding. The fire inside him blazed high enough to consume them both. The only problem was, she wanted a man who was husband and father material. Not one who overwhelmed her with passion, then responded to the siren call of a computer lab and disappeared for weeks on end.

"Charlie, will you for God's sake take care of yourself? When you come back, I don't want it to be as a pincushion." Dropping the receiver in place, Brand turned to Dena. "He's the only one I know who could drop by the nearest island for a friendly visit and find a tribe of spear-throwing natives."

He sat down beside her, disturbed by her expression. His bent fingers at her chin tilted her face to meet his. "You look sad, sweetheart. What's the matter?"

"Nothing," she lied, shifting to escape his scrutiny.

"Upset because you didn't match the writing?" His frown was perplexed. "You can't expect miracles, you know. I didn't think—"

Dena jumped to her feet and glared down at him. "If you say that you didn't expect me to accomplish anything one more time, I'm going to do something drastic. I already know that you're skeptical. I knew that from your writing, even before I met you."

The silence in the room seemed to ring with a voice of its own.

Brand stretched his legs out, crossing them at the ankles. He slid his hands into the pockets of his pants and looked at her. "I was going to say that I didn't think you'd do it the first day," he said quietly. That disposed of, he asked, "What writing?"

"I'm sorry," she said in a troubled voice. "This thing is driving me nuts. I don't know how you've handled the pressure for as long as you have."

He nodded, acknowledging her apology. "What writing?"

"Your initials," she muttered, wondering if she would ever learn to control her quick tongue around him.

"Where have you seen them?"

"On some of the forms John sent to me."

"And you learned what?"

She closed her eyes and sighed, knowing that he would keep at it all night if she didn't answer. "Your capital *b*. It's made with the upper bulb larger than the lower one, a classic sign of skepticism. So all of your doubts, while they've infuriated me, haven't surprised me a bit."

Eyeing his expressionless face, she sat down, leaving a cushion between them. He's probably a fantastic poker player, she decided in disgust, envying his ability to remain silent. When he finally turned to look at her, she wished she could read minds as well as handwriting.

"Anything else you want to tell me?" he asked politely.

Dena shook her head, reminding herself that discretion was the better part of valor. Not for anything, would she tell him about his capital *m*.

Brand stretched his arm across the cushion, holding out his hand. He waited until hers rested in it, then he rose, pulling her up with him. "It's been a long day for both of us. I'm going now."

Before they reached the door, he turned to face her. Taking a deep breath, he wrapped his arms around her and drew her against him. Their lips met just as the scented softness of her body leaned trustingly into his. God, but she felt good. His hands brushed her back, dropped to her waist, her hips, and settled on the tempting curve of her bottom, pressing her even closer. While the blood pounded in his head and his heart slammed against his chest, he was vaguely aware of Dena's arms twining around his neck, her hands lacing through his hair. At least she isn't running scared, he thought exultantly.

Brand's lips lifted and Dena sighed. Then they touched her eyebrow and temple. She tilted her face and smiled. The touch of his warm cheek, abrasive with a day's beard, could be addicting, she decided. With a sigh, she tugged at the back of his neck and brought his lips back to hers.

Later, still struggling for breath, he stepped back, keeping his hands on her shoulders. "The last thing in the world I want to do is walk away from you tonight. You know that, don't you?"

Speechless, she nodded.

"So I'm going to get out of here while I still can," he continued grimly. "Unless you want me to stay?" He saw the hesitation swirling in her amber gaze and knew he needed more than that. He wanted her running to him, making her own demands as well as meeting his.

Sighing sharply, he said, "I don't know what happened tonight to upset you, but give it time, will you? Together, we can work it out. Okay?" He waited for her nod, then stepped out and closed the door behind him.

Two days later, Dena leaned back and waited until Brand opened his door and slid behind the steering wheel. "So what do we do now?" she asked.

Two days of disappointment, she thought as he maneuvered out of the restaurant parking lot. Followed by disaster. She remembered how taut his voice had been when he called and asked her to come to his office shortly before quitting time. Jay Landry had been with him.

"Hi, guys. Why the glum faces?" Dena asked, closing the door behind her.

The two men looked up from the newspaper they were reading, their expressions grim.

"Have you seen this?" Brand asked.

"The paper? Nope. I work for a guy who's related to Simon Legree. He doesn't approve of reading on the job. That was a joke," she explained, when they scowled at her.

"Sit down." Brand waved at a chair and handed her the paper. "Read this," he said, pointing to an article on the first page.

It took only one glance to know why they were upset. It was an account of a forgery trial. A trial in which she had been a witness for the prosecution. Her evidence, so the paper said, helped convict the accused.

"Nice write-up. Rotten timing, though," Dean added mildly, folding the paper. "Any other time, I would have considered it good publicity." When no comment was forthcoming from either man, she continued. "I testified about ten days ago."

Jay cleared his throat. "Why didn't you tell us about it?"

"I forgot."

Brand snorted. "How could you forget something like that?"

"I've been court qualified for several years," Dena said calmly. "I'm frequently called on to prove the authenticity of documents. As far as I was concerned, it was just another case. I never thought of mentioning it. Besides, even if I had, what would you have done?"

"Changed your name, for starters," Brand said grimly. "Do you have any idea how many people at this company are going to read that article, remember your name, and realize why you're here?"

She looked at him in exasperation. "How many will really care?"

"It only takes one," Jay said in a quiet voice.

"You're really serious, aren't you?" Dena tilted her head, her smile fading as she watched the two men.

"A bit," Jay admitted.

"You might say that," Brand muttered at the same time.

"Hey, you two, ease up a little. I've never had anyone try to stop me from doing my job. No one's ever pulled a gun on me or resorted to kidnapping. I lead a very dull life," she finished.

"But how many people knew what you were doing?" Jay pointed out. "Most of your work is done confidentially, isn't it?"

"Well, yes, but—"

"That's what I thought." He nodded in satisfaction and turned to Brand. "How are we going to protect her? We'll have no trouble here, if she stays, because I'll assign one of my best men to her. But what about after hours?"

"I'll take care of that. Someone will be with her at all times."

Dena eyed the two of them in disbelief. It was a bit like watching storm clouds gather—fascinating, but totally beyond her control. She decided to make one more try.

"Look," she insisted, "I'll be okay. You aren't even *listening*," she said to two apparently deaf men.

Brand turned to her. His features could have been carved out of teak. "Because this time, you're out of your league. We're dealing with someone who's gone too far to stop. Someone who might easily decide you're a threat. Someone who, not inconceivably, will decide to remove the obstacle from his path.''

"We have to be careful, Dena," Jay added. "We can't take any chances. We don't know who we're dealing with.''

"What do you think Charlie would say if he knew about this?" Brand asked.

"Oh, God," Dena joked weakly, "don't even think of it. He'd quit annoying the locals and come back to mobilize the troops. Okay—" she sighed in surrender "—I don't believe for a minute that it's necessary, but if it'll make you feel better, I'll sign up for a bodyguard.''

Not liking the look on Brand's face, she added, "But don't think that you're going to hustle me out of here and wrap me in cotton until this is over. I'm going to be in the office downstairs every day until I find out who matches up with that writing.''

Now, slanting a look at the quiet man sitting next to her, she thought his expression hadn't changed much in the intervening hours. It was still hard, grim.

"Well," she repeated, "what do we do now?''

"I persuade you to come home with me so I don't spend the night wondering if you're all right.''

She blinked, leaning forward to look at his face. He was serious. "Brand, I can't do that," she began reasonably. "I'm not going to turn my life upside down just because someone *might* think this, or *may* do that. It's ridiculous. Besides, didn't you hire someone to sleep on my doormat all night?''

"Damn it, Dena—''

"Didn't you?''

"Yes.'' The word was a reluctant grunt.

"It's a sign of a good leader to delegate," she assured him. "You've done that; now you have to trust a little."

They were still arguing when he pulled to a stop at the curb. Slamming his door, he walked around to hers.

"If it will make you any happier, I'll let you come in and peek under the beds before you go home." Dena was about to add that he could also check the closets when a man stepped out from behind an oleander bush and scared the life out of her.

"Mr. McAllister?"

Before Dena could do more than gasp, Brand drew her to a halt, stepped in front of her and turned to confront the man. Her adrenaline was just rising to the occasion when she felt Brand's tension dissipate. He nodded.

"I'm Tom Norris from the agency. Looks like you waited too long to call me."

"What do you mean?" Brand asked tersely.

"Someone got in Miss Trevor's place before I came."

Dena stepped around Brand and looked at the other man. He was of average height and weight and had a face that was unremarkable. He was probably indispensable to the agency. He could follow anyone and never be seen. "How'd he get in?" she asked in bewilderment, thinking of her ritual of locking doors and windows.

"Miss Trevor," he said wearily, "the lock you have on your door wouldn't keep a baby out."

She decided not to tell him about the time she had locked herself out and needed to call a locksmith.

Brand grasped her elbow and started toward the door. "That settles it," he said grimly. "You're coming home with me."

Reserving judgment until she saw the house, Dena hurried down the walk.

Other than a couple of upended plants, the place didn't look too bad. Then she opened her office door. Sucking in her breath, she backed up into Brand. His arm wrapped around her waist, holding her against his warm body. The chilling sight before her made the warmth doubly welcome.

Her first thoughts centered around her books. She had spent weeks, sometimes months tracking some of them down. Old, out of print reference books, not expensive, perhaps, but hard to find. They were tumbled out of the oak bookshelves to the floor. Pages had been torn out, crumpled and thrown about the room. Pens and pencils were scattered all over, as if someone had taken a double handful and tossed them into the air.

It was merely a warning, she realized. If the person responsible had wanted to, there could have been far more destruction. There was no water or fire damage. Paint had not been splashed around. Actually, it was more of a mess than anything. Pages could be taped back in the books, and they could be replaced on shelves. Pens and pencils could be retrieved. No, she had lost nothing of material value, but she had been put on notice.

What was lost, perhaps irretrievably, was her sense of security. Her independence, her trust, her

problem thr
the plant. S
other kind
lice. Our co
and I'd like

"You mea
was a mistal

"No, it's
lie your way
as she bristle
want to tell t
we returned
broken in. O

"That's it

He nodde
stay at my h
many burgla
for some re
them you'r
don't menti
as someone

"Okay."

He leaned
her to her fe
assured her.

And there
They were
questions, v
work. No,
neighborho
hadn't notic
No, as far a
Yes, she wo

belief of invulnerability were all violated. She wondered sickly if she would ever again walk into her darkened home, trusting that all would be as she had left it. She doubted it.

Brand inhaled deeply. Turning her away from the door, he said, "Let's go check the other rooms."

She was grateful that there were no more shocks. The rest of the house was comfortably rumpled, the way she usually left it. The message was quite clear, she decided. The mysterious intruder had no grudge against her personally. But he—or she—was threatened by her work and wanted her to stop.

"I'll call the cops while you pack a bag," Brand said, nudging her toward her bedroom. He turned to Tom Norris and directed a few low-voiced comments to him before reaching for the telephone.

Dena left her door open while she collected her toothbrush and a few cosmetics. It wasn't that she was frightened, she told herself, she was...scared to death. She hadn't been exaggerating when she said she lived a dull life. Well, maybe not exactly dull, but certainly—at least up to now—without the excitement of breaking and entering. Rummaging through her lingerie, she pulled out bras and panties and dropped them in the small case on her bed. Enough for several nights, she decided, admitting that she was in no hurry to return. At least, not until the mysterious "X" was under restraint.

Selecting clothes slowed her down considerably. She needed things to work in, something more casual for evenings, but she didn't want to take so much that Brand might think she was staying indefinitely. Finally, she lifted out a versatile blue suit she often took on trips, added another skirt, two

blouses, sl
she change
That shoul

Carrying
time to wat

"Where

Brand r
her. "You
against his

"Nerves

"Where's

"To my

"Should

"I want
to a chair,
up in front
tively scoo

"What's t

"Not at
rubbing no
Speaking o
about to te
prompted,

He reacl
behind her

Now the
tated her b
ducing her
had known
like what h
that blunt

Her tone

Brand's
called the

ditional information. She saw them out and thanked them for coming.

Leaning back against the closed door, she let out a sigh of relief. "If you ever decide to live on the wrong side of the law, don't ask me to come along. I couldn't stand the tension. That was awful."

He patted her on the shoulder and grinned. "You did just fine. If you get a little more experience, Jay and I might let you sign up as a junior agent."

"Don't do me any favors," she said, moving away from the hand that slid down her arm and lingered on the soft flesh just above her elbow. Gently pulling away, she paced back to her suitcase wondering how on earth she had ended up in this mess. Living under the same roof with Brand McAllister was not going to be easy. She didn't trust the gleam in his eyes or, come to think of it, the satisfied expression on his face. Maybe a hotel would be—

"Dena, I thought you said you trusted me." He was leaning against the wall, his gray eyes glued on her expressive face.

Startled, she looked up at him, hoping that she didn't look as guilty as she felt. "I do," she said, wishing that her voice sounded firmer.

"Then you have nothing to worry about. You've put yourself into my hands, and you'll be safe there. As safe," he said slowly, "as you want to be."

She felt a surge of heat from her toes to her ears as he moved toward her. His hands settled on her shoulders, drawing her close until her head rested on his chest. It rumbled as he spoke.

"God knows there's nothing I'd like more than to take off your clothes and tuck you into my bed. But you'd have to want it as much as I do. So there'll be no pressure, no coercion. Of course," he said, leaning down and dropping a hard kiss on her lips, "I'm not saying I won't try to persuade you."

He left her to check the locks on the windows and doors and turn out the lights. "Are you ready?" he asked, his hand on the last switch.

For what? her active imagination asked.

He chuckled. "To go."

She nodded.

"When you're ready for more, let me know," he said, sweeping up the case and holding open the door.

During the short drive to his house, Dena's confused thoughts tumbled over one another. Regretting suddenly that she hadn't spent less time with textbooks and more practicing feminine wiles, she wondered how you inform a man of your decision when you are ready for the next step. Do you stand in front of him, tapping his shoulder to gain his attention, and blatantly announce the fact? Or would a smile do it? Or the look in her eyes? Good grief, her eyes *always* gave her away.

What if he misunderstood a perfectly innocent smile? What if he... Deciding that she was reaching panic and approaching paranoia, she gave herself stern instructions to calm down. Taking a few deep breaths helped.

Sooner than she believed possible, they turned into his driveway. He took her to the guest room, advised her to take a relaxing bath and turn in. She had, he informed her, had a rough evening.

For once, she followed his advice. As she lay in the firm, queen-size bed, she wondered if her imagination was working overtime. Had he, when he'd said goodnight, really looked down at her with a gleam in his eyes that up to now had been reserved for his precious equipment?

Chapter Nine

I don't know which one of you looks worse," Dena commented the next morning, looking at a weary Tom Norris and Red. Tom was rumpled and had pouches of exhaustion beneath his eyes; Red was doing a magnificent imitation of a dead dog.

"That damn dog—" Tom stared balefully at Red "—kept me throwing sticks all night. When I got here, Nick told me he'd bring him out and introduce us so Red would know I was a friend." He yawned until his jaws popped. "I think I'd rather be an enemy."

"Why didn't you go to bed?"

"Sentry duty," he said succinctly. "Night shift."

"You mean to say that with those two behemoths in here, you had to stay outside?"

Amusement gleamed in his eyes at her outraged expression. "That's how it is with us peons," he said. "We work all night while the rest of the world sleeps."

"That's awful," Dena said. "I had no idea you were coming here for that. I'm going to tell Brand—"

Tom sat up in alarm. "Hey, wait a minute. I was kidding. That's what I was hired—" Scrambling to his feet, he groaned, "Oh, no. Don't tell me we're having an earthquake."

Dena reached out to secure a tottering vase. "I think Nick is coming," she said dryly.

He stuck his head through the door, his gaze sliding over Dena and settling on Tom. "Breakfast's ready. In the kitchen." His head disappeared and Dena once again grabbed for the vase.

"You *do* see me, don't you?" she queried Tom. He nodded. "That man mystifies me," she said, glancing in the direction Nick had taken. "He never looks at me or talks to me. I'm beginning to get a complex."

They found Brand sitting at the table talking to Nick. "Anybody else call yesterday?" he asked.

Nick lunged for a hot pad and scooped scrambled eggs into a bowl. "Yeah. Samson's Construction. Said they ran into a problem with a couple of their backhoes and asked is it okay if they wait until Monday to finish the fish pond?"

"What fish pond?" Dena asked as Brand nodded affirmatively.

"Before Charlie left, we talked about turning a corner of the northeast field into a Japanese garden. We've already provided athletic facilities, so we wanted someplace quiet where people could go to relax. Samson's is doing the preliminary landscaping, moving dirt around to make hills and hollows. Unfortunately, in the process of scooping out the fishpond, they broke off a nearby sprinkler head and flooded the area. So what we have now is a mud pond surrounded by unpacked mounds of dirt. Thank God no one's using that area for anything right now.

"Tell them it's okay," he directed Nick. "Anything else?"

"Dog needs his rabies shot," he grunted. "Thought I'd take him in this afternoon. Since we're so close to the plant, is it okay if I let him run in the parkway for a while before I put him back in the car?"

Brand nodded absently and Tom muttered to Dena, "After last night, that dog shouldn't run for a week."

Dena watched Nick as he moved around the kitchen. The brawny man intrigued her. He didn't seem to dislike her, so why wouldn't he talk to her? She could tell when Nick became aware that her eyes were following him. His movements grew wilder, if that was possible. Finally, he thumped his way to the sink and busied himself with the dishes. She watched as a red tide crept up the back of his neck. I'll be damned, she thought with amazement, he's shy!

She was biting back a smile when Brand looked at his watch, then at her. "Ready to go?" he asked.

"Um-hmm. Just let me get my purse." She gulped down the last of her coffee, wiped her mouth with the napkin and stood up. As she passed Nick, she patted his arm. "Thanks for the breakfast, Nick. It was delicious."

His answer, which sounded something like "Snerff," was all but lost in the clatter of dishes.

Brand was waiting for her on the redwood deck which wrapped around the house. She stopped beside him. "Look at those gorgeous trees."

"They need pruning."

Dena glanced at him in exasperation. "You should let your brain shift to the right side more often."

His brows rose in inquiry. "What brought that on?"

"You did. I know that we need the left side of our brain to organize us and make logical decisions," she said, as if he had argued the point, "but if yours is telling you to prune the trees, it's ridiculous. If you were listening to your right side, it would suggest that you fill your lungs with this marvelous air and look at the stunning colors of the leaves. It certainly wouldn't advise you to lop off the branches so there'd be no leaves left."

"You're probably right," he said as they walked to the car.

She made a rude noise deep in her throat.

As they approached the plant, she asked, "Have you checked the names on that printout yet?"

"Uh-uh. Haven't had a chance."

"Someone's been left off. It just has to be that. I've checked every file I've been given and no one's writing has even come close to matching."

"I'll do it first thing," he promised.

"Great. Just jot down any names you think of," she suggested casually. "As soon as I get them, I'll have Millie pull the files."

"Okay." He didn't smile, so why did she have the feeling that he was amused?

Two hours later, she knew why.

John handed her an envelope. "I was just talking to Brand and mentioned that I would be dropping by. He sent this."

"Thanks." She dropped it on the desk and stared at it, barely listening to John. Could it be this easy, she wondered. Just tell him to jot down the names and he'd do it without thinking? Her fingers were fairly itching to tear open the envelope and pull out his note. She'd waited a long time to see more than a couple of scrawled initials.

"...seen Brand's mud puddle?"

Aware of his questioning tone, Dena responded absently. "No, but he told me about it." It had been a matter of principle, she told herself. Brand didn't believe in her work, so she wouldn't use any sneaky methods to get a sample of his writing. God knows it would have been easy enough. There must be tons of his notes floating around the place. No, she'd decided, he would have to give it to her. Hand it to her himself, so to speak. Of course, if he did it absentmindedly, she wasn't going to refuse a gift of the gods.

"...never seen anything like it. I suppose it won't be so bad when it's packed down and grass planted."

She nodded agreeably, reaching for the envelope and slitting it with a letter opener. She'd been nobility itself, she rationalized, holding off this long. She couldn't wait another minute to read his...typewritten note. *Typewritten*. And badly at that. There were crossed out words, some that ran together and others that had exotic spellings. He had obviously waited until Mrs. Hastings had left the office and used her typewriter. And, to add injury to insult, he had no information for her. The list, as far as he could see, was complete. He had no additional names for her. He was sincerely hers, etc. Damn and blast the man. Did he have any idea how maddening he was? Of course he did, she fumed.

So much for nobility and principles. If he was underhanded enough to send her a typewritten note, he deserved no further consideration. To think she had even been prepared to immediately close his file when she came upon it. His slanted writing was nothing like the vertical script on the note so she wouldn't have used the information in his file to satisfy her...

His file, she realized in growing wonder, she hadn't seen his file. And his name had to be on the list. It should have been *heading* the list. If his file wasn't there, how many others were missing?

"John." She sat back in her chair, ruthlessly interrupting his monologue. "When Millie pulled the folders for me, is it likely that she got them all on the first sweep?"

"I doubt it. Files are being pulled all the time for insurance and a lot of other reasons. If you walk out in the office right now, you'd see that there are some on every desk. We have strict rules about them leaving the office, but even so I can't guarantee that they're all here."

"What's her intercom number?" she asked, reaching for the phone.

A minute later, Millie walked in waving the printout. "There's about ten that I haven't been able to find. But I check for them each morning," she assured them.

"Let's see who they are," John said, holding out his hand. He unfolded the list and the three of them bent over the desk. Millie had neatly checked off each name as she pulled the file. Dena's eyes widened at the sight of a blank space near the top. Millie had not located records for three of the five engineers with whom Brand was working: Art Dexter, Karen Michaels and Burt Silver. People who were right in the middle of things and had more opportunity than most to walk out with information. She looked up, her eyes meeting John's speculative gaze. They exchanged nods and returned to the list. None of the other names were familiar to Dena.

Millie left the office promising to find the missing files if she had to search every desk in the building. "If you see me running down the hall with a crowd at my heels, I expect you to protect me," she informed John over her shoulder as she left.

John's grin faded as he turned back to Dena. "What do you think?"

"I think it looks a lot more encouraging than it did yesterday." She slid her hands into the pockets of her blue jacket and stared out the window. "I've thought all along that it had to be someone fairly close to the top."

Turning back to face John, she said abruptly, "I'm going up to see Brand. If I accidently run into some of those engineers on the way, I think I'll stop and get better acquainted." She walked to the elevator, mentally sifting through the various possibilities and didn't even notice the man behind her who slid through the doors just before they closed.

While Dena was staring at the panel of buttons in the elevator, Brand was frowning at a stack of papers on his desk. His frown was directed not so much at the papers as at himself. His attitude. Normally, he thrived on facing problems begging for solutions. Devoured them and looked around for more. But, he checked his watch, he'd been here for over two hours and hadn't managed to absorb the information on one single page.

How, he asked himself, tossing a pencil down in disgust, could a man concentrate when a woman was traipsing around the place looking and asking for trouble. Especially when it was a stubborn, delectable, sexy-as-hell woman. *His* stubborn, delectable, sexy-as-hell woman. If she was in her office, where she was supposed to be, she was still vulnerable. Even with one of Jay's best men hovering behind a potted plant down the hall. Why on earth was there just one? What could one do if she really needed help?

He reached for the phone, intending to ask Jay that very question, when someone tapped lightly on the door.

"Hi, are you busy?"

At the sight of Dena's smiling face, Brand let the receiver drop. "Come in." His eyes followed her every move as she sat down, relishing her presence after his flare of anxiety. "Did you get my message?" he asked.

She tilted her head thoughtfully. "Which one was that? Ah, the typewritten one? Indeed I did." Her eyes were a shimmering blend of green and gold. "Dirty trick, McAllister. But then I should have expected it from someone who makes his capital *m* the way you do."

His eyes gleamed at her humorous tone. "And you can't wait to tell me what's wrong with it, can you?"

"Nothing's wrong with it," Dena assured him. "There's no good or bad writing, just different. But making the last upper stroke higher than the first two simply tells me that you're a man who asserts himself when it's least expected. You're also one who prefers a position of authority, is stubborn, and tenacious when going after something you want."

He nodded, as if it were a fair analysis. "You'd do well to remember that," he recommended.

"Now why does that sound like a threat?" she wondered aloud.

"Merely a suggestion." Warmth stirred low in his body as he met her speculative gaze. Soon, he decided, they were going to settle this thing between them. Their reckoning would come once this mess was cleared away and she could concentrate on something besides samples of writing. How she managed to do that still mystified him. These days, his brain—both right and left sides—had about as much animation as a dish of yogurt.

His frank gaze swept over her. Past her honey-blond hair, warm lips, and teasing glances to a body designed for a man's hands and arms. A classy lady; a warm, loving woman. His woman. It no

longer surprised him that he thought in terms of
ownership, of possession. He had claimed her, she
was his. Typically, his mind turned to the next step,
making her realize and accept the fact. After that,
they would inform the world. He didn't care if it
was done with labels on her clothes or a diamond
ring—a large one. As long as it was done.

Dena returned his glance as calmly as she could,
wondering what he was thinking. If only he weren't
so quiet, she thought for the hundredth time. Once
this thing is over, she was definitely going to do
something about that. She wasn't going to spend
the rest of her life wondering what was going on
inside his head. He would just have to learn to talk.
She blinked, watching his expression change. It
was, she realized, one thing to plan for the future,
entirely another to cope with the present, and that
hungry look.

After clearing her throat, Dena spoke rapidly. "I
dropped in to see if it's all right if I go talk to your
five engineers again?"

He examined her expression thoughtfully. "Have
you come up with something?" he asked.

"Not really. Millie is trying to run down the last
of the files. I have yet to see those belonging to
three of the famous five. I'm just prowling around
while I'm waiting."

"And they're the logical ones to prowl around,
right?"

She nodded reluctantly, hating to make prema-
ture judgments.

He sighed. "I know. Jay and I keep coming back
to them even though we haven't found a thing."

"Is it okay?" she asked, getting up from the chair.

He followed her to the door. "Dena?"

"Hmm?"

"Be careful."

She looked up, startled at his serious tone. "I will," she promised, nodding solemnly.

He leaned down, touching her lips lightly with his, then opened the door.

An hour later, Dena closed the tenth file with a sigh of frustration. Nothing. Absolutely nothing. Idly tapping a pencil against the edge of her desk, she thought of her trip upstairs. Talking to the five, collectively and individually, had not helped a bit. Despite Charlie's belief in her, she had experienced no nuances, no vibes. Nothing made her suspect that they were anything but what they seemed to be.

If any of them were miscast, it was Burt Silver. He had the personality of a salesman or promoter, but he must be a better than average engineer or he wouldn't be here. Brand was not the type to suffer fools, gladly or otherwise. Burt was quick to see the humor of a situation and laughed more easily than the others. She smiled, remembering how he had teased Wayne about his new Porsche, commenting that the company was in a bad way if it felt obligated to reward such puny efforts. Wayne had merely replied that good companies recognized good employees, smoothed his mustache and returned to work.

The rhythm of the tapping pencil grew slower as Dena's eyes widened. Staring at the closed door as if any moment a printed solution to her problem would appear on its smooth surface, she frowned in thought. There *was* something. A personality quirk that had been nagging at her subconscious for days, but it was so farfetched...

Millie's curly head poked through the open door. "Can I hide in here?" she asked in a hoarse whisper.

"What on earth's the matter?" Dena couldn't help smiling at the woebegone expression on the other woman's face.

"I'm doomed," she groaned, closing the door. "Just let me curl up in a corner until I get the nerve to face him."

"Who? I mean whom?"

"John, that's whom."

"That nice man?"

"That nice man is a Jekyll and Hyde. He grows fangs and prowls at midnight when someone loses material from a file. And that's just what I've done."

Smiling at the exaggeration, Dena soothed, "I'll help you find it."

Millie shook her head dismally. "It's not that easy. I have it here," she waved a sheet of paper in front of Dena. "When I moved all those files for you, it fell out. The problem is, I don't know where it goes. It looks like the second page of a letter and there's no name on it. He will absolutely, positively kill me. But first, he'll fire me."

"Let me see." Dena held out her hand.

Millie released the paper with a flip of her wrist and watched gloomily as it drifted to a stop in the center of the desk.

Dena's amused smile froze as she looked down at the precise, vertical script. She had almost begun to think it was a figment of her imagination, but there it was with its excessive upstrokes shouting of resentment, the down slanted line that often spoke of depression, knots of secretiveness, and the blunt finals slanting downward that told of smoldering emotions. After scanning the message, she sighed, sharing Millie's frustration. It was an angry letter about the parking lot, rendered senseless by its missing pages.

"Millie, would you leave this with me for a while? I'll take care of it for you."

Intrigued by Dena's serious expression, she nodded and got up. "I'm depending on you to protect me," she reminded the younger woman.

"I'll do that," Dena murmured absently. Staring at the paper, she wondered at the perversity of a fate which finally allowed her to find the writing, yet still concealed the identity of the writer. She opened a drawer and lifted out a magnifying glass.

An hour later, she leaned back in the chair. It would take hours to do a complete analysis, but she was willing to work in reverse and take an educated guess. So far, of those she had met, one person fit the emerging picture.

Moving slowly, as if a sudden motion would shatter her tenuous thoughts, Dena opened the door and walked over to the bank of four-drawer files. She searched methodically, checking entire drawers to make sure the folder had not been misplaced. Nothing. A feeling of urgency suddenly gripped her. Not for a minute did she believe that there was an innocent explanation for the disappearance of this folder.

Seconds later she was picking up her phone and dialing. Swinging around in the swivel chair, she stared at the wall behind her desk and waited. Deliberately she took a deep, steadying breath and closed her eyes. On the third ring, he answered.

"Brand? I think someone has been playing games with the files I've been checking. Will you do something for me?" She bit back impatient words as he interrupted. Finally, she said, "Will you find something written by each of your five engineers? It doesn't matter what it is, anything will do. I'm coming right up. 'Bye." Swinging the chair back, Dena replaced the receiver, opened her eyes...and released her breath in a long, controlled sigh.

Wayne Randall stood before her. "I was afraid something like this might happen," he said.

Strange, she thought in surprise, he doesn't look any different. Still shockingly handsome, quiet, a bit too serious. And pensive. Not at all like a high-tech thief should look. He should appear threatening, even violent. Not as if nothing had changed. For she was, she realized sadly, looking at a man whose world was falling to pieces. Her sympathy was killed at birth by his next statement.

"But when you plan something like this, you allow for a certain amount of risk." His expression didn't alter as he looked down at her.

"I gather that you saw the newspaper article?"

He nodded and rested one hip on the corner of her desk. "Up to that time I bought your foundation story. You should have paid attention to my warning, you know."

"My office?" She swallowed nervous laughter that was forming in her throat. From his tone, she thought, he could have been chiding her for ignoring a suggestion to wear sun-tan lotion when going to the beach.

He nodded again. "It would have been simpler all around if you had."

"Wayne—" she leaned forward "—it's not too late to—"

"Because now I have to do something about you."

Smothering an impulse to apologize, Dena asked, "Why did you do it?"

He shrugged. "Additional retirement, burnout. Look around, you'll see it all over this area. Men working so many hours under high pressure that they're used up before they hit their forties."

"Wayne," she tried again, "now is the time to stop—"

"I think we'd better be on our way." His voice was casual.

"Where?" she asked numbly.

"To my car."

She remembered telling Brand that she wasn't a TV heroine. Truer words were never spoken. Keeping her voice steady wasn't easy, but she managed. "I'd be crazy to step out of this office with you."

He shook his head. "You don't really have much choice."

"How do you figure?"

"Because I've got a gun and you don't."

In the silence that followed, Dena sifted through her options. It seemed, despite Jay and his famous cameras, a Security person who was supposed to be hovering around her, Brand, Nick, Tom and the dog, she was on her own. She was also terrified. She almost leaped out of her chair when the telephone pealed at her elbow. Her gaze lifted to the cool-blue eyes of the man across from her.

He reached in his pocket and pulled out a small, but very nasty-looking gun. "Answer it," he said. He reached over, his hand covering hers on the receiver. "And, Dena, be careful. Anyone who gets between us and the car will get hurt."

She nodded, never lifting her eyes from the gun being pointed at her. Clearing her throat, she lifted the receiver. "Hello."

"Dena? I thought you were coming right up." Brand sounded as if he were in the same room. The realization that he would be, should he detect a shread of fear in her voice, galvanized Dena. The adrenaline surged through her body and became a positive force, nudging her into action.

Her voice apologetic, she said, "I'm sorry, Brand. Something came up. Give me about fifteen minutes, will you?"

"I thought you were in such a hurry," he said, puzzled.

"I was. I am," she said, rapidly sensing Wayne's impatience. "Fifteen minutes, okay?" Dropping the receiver, she stood up, automatically reaching for her purse. "All right, Wayne, I'm ready if you are."

He slid to his feet, weighing her reaction. "Why the sudden rush?"

She flexed her shoulders, easing the tension. Her eyes, when she looked at him, were clear and honest. "Because there are a lot of people out there who would try to help me if they thought I needed it. I don't want anyone getting hurt."

He slid the gun in the pocket of his jacket and dropped an arm around her shoulder. "Okay. If anyone stops us, make it clear that you're with me because you want to be." She nodded, her expression frozen.

When they stepped into the outer office, she looked straight ahead, wondering what Brand would think when she didn't show up. Halfway through the room she passed a man sitting at a desk gazing thoughtfully over her head. She paid no attention when he reached for the phone and spoke quietly.

Chapter Ten

Brand stared at the report on his desk and swore with quiet emphasis. He had read it four times and still didn't know what the damn thing was about. He shifted his gaze to the silent telephone. There was nothing to worry about, he reminded himself. She was in her office with Jay's top man posted outside. A quick glance at his watch assured him. Two minutes since he had talked with her. Thirteen more and she'd be walking through the door.

A frown drew his heavy brows together. Had her voice sounded strained when he called her? He swore again. It had not. It was just his imagination. Now that would amuse her, Brand McAllister letting his imagination run wild. He checked his watch again. Four minutes. What if she finished whatever she was doing early? Would she think she had to wait the full fifteen minutes? He thought about it. Probably. Wouldn't hurt to let her know she could come up whenever she was ready. He reached for the phone just as it rang.

"Brand?" Jay's voice was so uncharacteristically terse Brand's nerves tightened. "We've got an emergency situation down here and I think you'd better sit in on it."

"Is it our man?"

"Probably. But we've got a...complication. Make it as soon as you can, will you?"

That request, Brand thought as he ran to the elevator, coming from Jay was the equivalent of a full-scale alarm with red lights flashing and sirens howling. Two minutes later, he was walking into a hive of well-orchestrated activity.

"Over here, Brand." Jay was pressing buttons and giving low-voiced directives, all the while keeping tabs on the various monitors. Brand glanced up at the nearest screen—and froze.

Bleak gray eyes flicked over the other monitors. His breath backed up in his lungs when he saw Randall's arm draped over her shoulder. Inhaling deeply, he asked, "Where are they?"

Jay eyed him thoughtfully and with a raised brow deployed two men to cover the door. His voice was quiet. "Why?"

"Because," Brand said calmly, "I'm going to find the bastard and kill him." After staring intently at the monitors, he nodded and swung on his heel.

Jay's words stabbed at him like blades of tempered steel. "All you'll succeed in doing is getting *her* killed. Damn it, man, she needs you *right here*."

Brand stopped just short of the door. He lifted his arm and put a hand on the wall. Staring at the floor, he exhaled sharply. When he had control of himself, he looked up at Jay. "What do you want me to do?"

Turning away from the raw look in his eyes, Jay said softly, "Just stay here, out of range, and don't put her in any danger."

Brand's voice stopped him. "Out of range? He has a gun?"

"We don't know. We have to assume that he does. *My* men are armed. If necessary they're prepared to shoot when we can assure Dena's safety." A quick glance assured him that Brand was listening. "Right now, they're in a net of our people. As they move along, they'll be in a loose circle of guards. Having this advantage—" he waved at the monitors "—we can keep one step ahead of them. We don't want Randall to panic. The longer he thinks he's unobserved, the safer Dena will be. If he sees no signs of activity, he just may hang around while he figures out his next step."

Brand's gaze was drawn back to a screen that had a close-up of Dena. Her eyes closed as she drew in a shuddering breath. Then she and Randall stepped into an elevator. The doors closed behind them and their image faded from the screens.

Being alone and independent isn't all that it's cracked up to be, Dena decided as she walked beside Wayne.

She'd give a year's salary and toss in her favorite potted fern just to feel Brand's arm around her waist right now. What would he do if he *were* here?

she wondered. Probably the same thing she was doing. Play for time, talk, and if given the opportunity, run like hell. Despite all the talk about sexual equality, she thought, when things got rough, there was still something tremendously reassuring about a man's physical strength.

Even knowing that someone down in Security had watched her leave with Wayne didn't help. After all, it wasn't as if he had dragged her away at gunpoint. Nothing about their leave-taking had been noteworthy enough to attract attention. That was exactly how she had wanted it—no panic, no one hurt.

Her reasoning hadn't changed, just her attitude. It was easier to be brave inside a building surrounded by people. Outside, with the sun spreading its warmth over them and only an occasional car passing by, her actions seemed harder to justify. Wincing, she mentally rehearsed her explanation to Brand. That was going to be cute. Assuming, of course, that she got out of this mess alive. For a moment, the alternative didn't seem all that bad.

Certainly, she would say, she hadn't wanted an innocent bystander injured. And...and what? There wasn't anything else. She'd just have to play that one up for all it was worth. The only other reason she had—and never to her dying day would she admit it to Brand—was that with her training as a psychologist, she believed she could reason with Wayne. She was sure the situation wouldn't escalate to the point of violence. But, as someone once said, facts is facts.

Fact number one, she reminded herself, was that the man next to her had a gun. Following right on its heels was the realization that, if cornered, he might just use it. On her. Dena had never owned a gun, never even handled one. But she had watched enough television to know that bullets made ugly holes in people. Holes that were difficult to patch up and painful to heal. All in all, it was an experience she could do without.

Wayne slid off the car cover, folded it neatly and stowed it away. He rubbed an invisible blemish on one fender with his pristine handkerchief before opening the door for Dena. Sliding behind the wheel, he inserted the ignition key and stared thoughtfully at it. Sighing sharply, he leaned back and ran his fingers through his thick blond hair.

"I gather I'm an unexpected complication," Dena observed quietly.

Slanting a wry look at her, he nodded agreement. "I don't want to hurt you," he said quietly. "Hell, I don't want anyone to get hurt. But if push comes to shove, I'll take care of myself. Any way that I have to." His hand dropped unconsciously to his pocket.

Chilled by the quiet gesture, Dena took a steadying breath. "Wayne, no one else knows what's taken place between us. Nothing has changed as far as the people back there—" she nodded at the building "—are concerned. Can't we go somewhere and talk? Before you get in so deep that there's only one way out?"

Wayne's glance was skeptical. "You think it hasn't already reached that point?"

"I know it," she said with more confidence than she felt. "You pick the place, wherever you want to go." Her breath went out with a silent rush when he reached out and turned the key.

It's such a waste, she thought angrily. If she could have found his records on the first day, before he decided that kidnapping and using a gun would solve things, she might have been able to help him.

"Why couldn't I find your file?" she asked curiously as he eased out of the parking slot.

"I took it," he said briefly.

"When?"

"The first morning you were in the office."

She looked at him thoughtfully. "That doesn't make sense. You told me you bought my cover story, and the newspaper article hadn't come out yet. There was nothing to alarm you. Besides, I was there talking to you. How could you take it?"

He glanced at her then returned his eyes to the road ahead. "My first visit was when you were on a break. Actually, I just dropped in to say hello, and I saw my file on your desk. It was about the third one from the top."

"But what made you take it? As far as you knew, I was just gathering statistics."

His features were grim when he answered. "Once you cross the line, you get a bit paranoid. I didn't care what you were doing, I didn't want you checking my file. I just tucked it in with some papers I was taking to another office. On my way back, you had returned and I stopped in for a few minutes."

"As simple as that," she murmured. They had left the parking lot behind and were heading for the far corner of the complex. It all looked so peaceful, she thought, as they drove past a hollow of brightly hued foliage. Leaves were spiraling to the ground with the aid of a gentle breeze, the sun enhancing their changing colors.

Pulling her mind away from the pastoral serenity, Dena looked at the man beside her, wondering if he would stop before he left the company property. The road they were on, she remembered, led to the athletic field, the construction area, and an access road leading to the freeway. Her stomach lurched at the possibility of blending in with the city traffic and traveling to an unknown destination with a man who was, to put it mildly, up to his armpits in alligators.

Wayne surprised her by making a series of sharp turns and coming to a stop on the verge of a grassy knoll overlooking a mud hole. Even at a time like this, she noted, he had pulled neatly on the last scrap of grass. It was, she knew, the future home of the Japanese garden, but it looked more like a location for a war movie. Dirt had been scooped out here and dumped there in a loose knit pattern around the muddy crater that would eventually be a fish pond.

Wayne got out of the car and stood by the open door. Dena followed suit, silently joining him.

"How deep in this mess are you?" she asked abruptly.

"How deep can you get?" The words were heavy.

"Can you stop it?"

"Can you stop the tide?"

"Don't go poetic on me," she said with irritability. "And quit answering my questions with more questions. I'm serious."

In the silence that followed, Wayne took off his jacket and draped it over the open door. It settled with a thud, reminding Dena of the revolver in his pocket. Her startled gaze met his.

The blue of his eyes deepened. "Don't worry, Dena. If I use it on anyone, it'll probably be myself."

"Somehow, that isn't very comforting," she said in a tight voice. "I asked if you could stop this whole thing."

Deliberately moving away from the gun, she stepped toward the front of the car and ran her finger along the silver fender as she waited for his answer. Her eyes lit with satisfaction as he followed, whipping out his handkerchief to remove her handiwork.

"Yes," he said finally. "I could stop it. But it won't do me any good. Brand knows what's going on. The fact that you're on the job proves that. Once he finds out I'm the one he's been looking for, it'll be all over. Even if I don't end up in jail, I'll never get a decent job again."

"How on earth did you get involved in this mess?" Dena's voice carried no accusation. Whatever happened, he wouldn't use that gun on anyone, she vowed silently. Especially himself.

"Mess is right." He pocketed his handkerchief and stared down at the mud. "A couple of months ago we thought we were on to something in the lab and we worked like maniacs. The possibility of a breakthrough of any kind is like that," he explained. "The stimulation keeps you going. I wouldn't go home. Kept thinking that any minute I'd come up with a solution. Instead, I crashed. Total exhaustion followed by a hellish depression. I kept working, but I thought the company owed me. Even when I got this baby—" he patted the fender "—it didn't satisfy me." He shook his head slowly. "I decided that if they wouldn't give me what I deserved, I'd take it. It was that simple, that crazy."

"Sounds like burnout to me," Dena said evenly. Would she ever understand an industry that devoured the very people who created it? Would she ever understand what drove those same people to their limits, and beyond? With a frustrated sound, she turned away.

An excited yelp brought her head around. A flash of color pinned her gaze to the sweeping expanse of lawn to her right. Several hundred yards away, Red was retrieving a Frisbee thrown by Nick. He galloped back with it and quivered with excitement as Nick wound up for another throw. Dena smiled as he darted away, anticipating the toss. Tearing down the lawn, Red leaped up, diverting the plastic disc with his body. Snatching it off the ground, he pranced back to Nick.

Clapping her hands, Dena called out, "Good for you, Red. You're a clever boy!" She waved as Nick looked up. He raised his hand in acknowledgment.

At the sound of her voice, Red forgot his game and turned, searching for Dena. He gave a wuff of anticipation when he spotted her. Ears flapping in the wind and plumed tail straight out behind him, he made a beeline for her. It was that exact moment, Dena decided later, that her situation changed from alarming to ludicrous.

Before she finished saying to Wayne, "Look, there's Brand's dog," Red had arrived. Cavorting around them in a loose figure eight pattern he whined his delight.

"Yes, you're a good dog," Dena assured him, warding him off with both hands. "Go make friends with Wayne," she said, pointing at her serious companion. "Maybe he'll throw a stick for you."

Enthusiastically following her pointing finger, Red leaped to the hood of the car and poked his moist black nose in Wayne's ear. Wayne's stunned gaze followed the dancing paws and the trail of dusty prints they left behind. "Damn it," he roared, "get off my car!"

Dena held her breath, blessing that brainless dog. For someone who hadn't been sure that she would be alive at lunchtime, things were definitely looking up. And, she decided, if ever there was a time to move, it was now!

Keeping an eye on Wayne and Red, who had apparently decided that he was being introduced to a new game, she reached for the jacket and dug in the pocket for the gun. Wayne spun around, forgetting the dog.

"Give me the jacket, Dena," he ordered.

She backed away, brushing the back fender with her leg. Wayne advanced cautiously, his hand outstretched. Red whined.

"Come on, Dena, give it to me." Visibly containing his anxiety, Wayne moved closer.

Dena shook her head, backing down the slope. Pulling the gun free of the pocket, she tossed the jacket to Wayne. He snagged it with a long arm and threw it aside. Red stood on the fender, poised for action.

Stalking her, Wayne said gently, "I need the gun, Dena."

"Uh-uh," she panted. "I'll do a lot for you, but not that." Sliding one foot behind, Dena tested the ground before shifting her weight. She also spared a moment to dream of Nick thundering over the hill, flexing his muscles and tattoos and taking charge. Forget it, she told herself. Nick can't see through hills or cars. You're on your own, so think!

Wayne stopped, eyeing her in exasperation. "Damn it," he said, "will you listen to reason?"

Dena ignored him, gauging the distance to the tip of the knoll and the mud beyond. If she could throw it hard enough to bury it— Wayne lunged at her, abruptly ending the review of her options. Dena lobbed the gun in an underhand toss. It soared above Wayne's raised arm in a graceful arc. It was a good throw, she thought dispassionately. A very good throw. Unfortunately, Red was watching and thought so too. With an excited yelp, he launched himself from the fender. Like a guided missile, he found his target and deflected it with his body. Instead of landing down in the mud, it fell to the ground at the tip of the knoll.

Sidestepping Wayne's rush, Dena dashed for the top of the sloping hill. The heavy thud of his feet was close behind her. He was quick, she granted, too quick for his own good. She snatched the gun from the grass, wound up for another throw and tumbled to the ground as Wayne's shoulders hit the back of her knees. With a high pitched bark, Red landed on top of them.

"Get him, Red!" she yelled.

Wayne shouldered the dog away as he tried to pin her to the ground. "Damn it, Dena," he panted, "just give me the damned gun."

His efforts were hampered by the fact that he wouldn't hurt her. She realized this and took full advantage of it. Squirming away, she rolled over and looked up into Red's snapping amber eyes. "Go get him!" she commanded.

Red was willing, but confused. He jumped between them, then turned to swipe at Dena's face with a long moist tongue.

"You wretch," she gritted, and slung the gun back over her head where, with any luck at all, it would land in the mud. He wuffed and leaped after it.

"No!" She raised herself on one elbow. "I didn't say *fetch,* you stupid dog. Come back here!"

She fell back with a groan and turned to face Wayne. "Football?" she asked with a raised brow.

"High school," he admitted, "and college."

She sighed. "Figures."

"Why'd you do it?" He pointed beyond the crest of the knoll where Red was out of sight, snuffling energetically.

"I wasn't going to give you a gun that you might decide to use on yourself."

He smiled with gentle mockery. "Miss Dogooder. You're going to save me in spite of myself."

"Yeah. I'm compulsive that way. I can't stand seeing people mess up—" Her eyes widened as the ground beneath them shifted. "My God, what was that? Don't tell me we're having an earthquake."

He rolled to his feet in a lithe movement, reached out a hand and pulled her up beside him. Looking around with a puzzled frown, he said, "I don't think so. It felt different. It was almost—"

His words broke off so suddenly Dena looked up in alarm. She followed his fixed stare over the top of the car. They both stooped down and looked through the two open doors to the mounds of dirt beyond. A magnificently muddy Red had apparently overcome his natural reluctance to retrieving a metallic object and was barreling back to them. Unless diverted, his arrow-straight return would take him through the passenger door and out the driver's side of the car.

"No!" Wayne thundered. "By God, dog, you do that and I'll break your neck."

Dena bit back a nervous giggle. He wouldn't hurt the dog. She was jeopardizing his entire future and he hadn't harmed her. But Red, she realized belatedly, was treading on delicate ground. He was menacing Wayne's *car*.

Dena prudently backed away. The threat had done little to alter Red's direction. In fact, she thought, the dog looked as if he had just received an encouraging call and was moving faster than ever. His paws touched the seat she had been occupying such a short time before, then he gathered himself for one last bound out the other side.

Wayne had not moved away. The dog's weight hit him squarely in the chest and he tumbled backward. Dena winced and slowly opened her eyes. Wayne was lying on his back with Red's paws planted on his chest. Red opened his mouth and dropped the gun by Wayne's ear, his matted tail fanning back and forth.

Inarticulate with rage, the downed man rose to his feet. He speared a look at the muddy swath on the fabric of the seats and grabbed for the dog. Red frisked away, obviously delighted with his new friend. Trembling with laughter, Dena watched as Red darted forward and dropped down, front legs and nose resting on the ground, his rear end elevated with his tail cutting circles in the air. She shifted her attention to Wayne.

Wayne was not amused. Muttering, he swiped at the dog and watched in disgust as he leaped over the hood of the car. Turning to Dena, he said, "I swear to God, I'll—" Alarm replaced the fury in his eyes.

"What's the matter?" Dena began, then her gaze followed his to the ground.

"Move back," he ordered in an urgent voice.

She retreated, watching in disbelief as the turf beneath the front tires began to sink. At first it looked as if gophers were nibbling the roots of the grass; small strips along the edge fell and disappeared. Soon dirt clods and chunks of grass were vanishing from the knoll, clattering down the slope.

Wayne swore softly. "They must have gouged some dirt out of this hill and the ground is still shifting."

Dena gasped as the front tires slowly settled, changing the angle of the car, until the front was pointed directly down at the pool of mud. She looked at Wayne and noticed the stubborn flexing of his jaw muscle.

"I may have lost my job and ruined my entire future—" he gritted between his teeth "—but I'm not...going...to...lose...this...car. Dena, go sit on the back, will you? Don't worry," he assured her, noticing her startled look, "if it starts moving, I'll get you off. I just want to see if the shift in weight will help."

It wasn't the most flattering statement in the world, she thought in amusement as she eased herself onto the car. But then he had more on his mind than pandering to her ego. She inhaled sharply as the car slipped another notch.

"I don't think this is working," she told him. "You're heavier than I am, why don't you sit back here too?"

He settled beside her, angling himself so he could see the front of the car. "Okay, boss. Now what?"

"I think you should stay here while I go for help." Gold-flecked eyes met blue ones for a long moment. "But I'll only do it if you want me to," she said.

"You might as well," he finally said. "I don't know of any other way out of this." They both knew he wasn't talking about the car.

She reached out and touched his hand. "Wayne, it'll be all right. At least, I think so," she added honestly. Sliding down, she kicked off her shoes and began to run.

How far was it back to the building, she wondered. Could she get there before the car slid to the bottom? Maybe she'd run into someone on the way. Anybody with a car and a rope would do. Or maybe several brawny men without a rope. As long as she was wishing, what about a tow truck?

Dashing around a tight corner, she skidded to a halt. There before her, lined side by side across the road, were six security cars. Jay, Brand, and Nick were standing apart from a knot of men who looked up as she approached. The three men turned to face her.

"Is this the posse?" she asked weakly.

Chapter Eleven

Dena! Thank God." Strong arms wrapped around her. "Are you all right?"

Her head was pressed against Brand's shoulder. She shook it. "No."

His arms tightened, pulling her closer. "What's the matter?" he asked in a tight voice.

"You're cracking my ribs," she gasped.

He set her on her feet and looked at her. Even with her hair falling in her smudged face, a torn skirt and stockings, she was the most beautiful thing he had ever seen. "I want you to know," he stated grimly, "that I've just spent the worst morning of my life. What in sweet hell have you been up to?"

"Oh, I've been having a wonderful time," she told him, noting with interest that his composure had cracked. He was not quiet anymore. In fact, his last question had been delivered at a full-throated roar. "I was kidnapped at gunpoint, almost lost a wrestling match, got kissed by a dog, and watched the ground disappear from beneath my feet. And all before lunch."

She turned to Jay. "You can put the arsenal away. He doesn't have the gun anymore. I threw it in the mud."

He eyed her in fascination. "When?"

"After the wrestling match," she decided. Looking accusingly at Brand, she added, "Just as your lunatic dog appeared on the scene and insisted on retrieving the blasted thing."

"Where is he?" Brand gritted through clenched teeth.

"Back there—" she waved in the general direction "—driving Wayne crazy."

"Not the dog, damn it, *Randall.*

Dena looked up into arctic-gray eyes. Eyes that were giving off warning signals. Eyes the color of...Wayne's car!

"Oh my gosh." She ran a hand through her hair. "I'm supposed to be getting help."

"You are. We're it," Jay reminded her quizzically.

"Not for me," she explained, her voice raising. "Wayne's sitting on the back of his car to keep it from sliding into the mud."

"What?" The other men stopped talking and moved in closer. "You mean Randall's Porsche?" one of them asked.

She nodded.

"The one that he won't let anyone touch?" another queried.

Jay studied the expression on her face as she nodded again. "What else is wrong with it?" he asked.

"Aside from Brand's dog wallowing in the mud then jumping in it, nothing at all," Dena said straight-faced.

A snicker broke the stunned silence. "This I've got to see," said an awed voice.

A tall redhead grinning from ear to ear approached Jay. "Boss, don't you think some of us ought to help him out?" The others stepped forward to volunteer.

Jay's voice was dry. "Your concern really touches me, but—" He stopped and looked at Brand. Dena intercepted the query.

"Please, let them go," she requested in a voice meant only for the two men. "He'll come back with them." She raised pleading eyes to Brand. "Please? He needs your help." She hadn't realized how tense she was until Brand and Jay exchanged glances.

"I say let them go and bring him back here," Brand said, "but you're in charge of this operation. It's up to you."

Dena's beseeching gaze shifted to the other man. Holding her breath, she was vaguely aware of Nick's green eyes examining her.

"I hope we don't regret this," Jay muttered. Within seconds Nick and the others piled into a pickup and turned onto the dirt road. Dena sighed as the two remaining men each cupped a hand on her shoulder and led her over to one of the cars. Brand's hands settled at her waist, and lifted, settling her on the fender. "Okay, tell us everything that happened," Jay commanded.

Five minutes later, it was her turn to ask questions. "How did Nick find you here?"

Brand's answer was short. "When Red ran to you Nick decided to tag along. He came along the road and ran into us. We were afraid he'd barge in and set Randall off so we told him to stay put. Almost had to tie him down to keep him here." He watched her as she turned to Jay. Had she been hurt? Was she keeping something from him in order to protect Randall? His stomach muscles contracted as another question surfaced. Did she feel something more than sympathy for him?

"So what made you think Randall was the leak?" Jay was asking.

Dena frowned, her words slow and thoughtful. "Every time I saw him, I got confused messages. His body language was ambivalent whenever he spoke of the company." She put a hand on Brand's shoulder to balance herself as she shifted to a more comfortable position.

"It reminded me of the way that children react," she told them. "When they lie, they often cover their mouths. In adults, it's a bit more sophisticated, but they still have that instinct to touch their mouths. In Wayne's case, almost every time he mentioned the company, he smoothed his mustache." Shrugging, she admitted, "It was a small thing but pretty consistent."

She broke off, gazing over Jay's shoulder. The small army, dirty but triumphant, was returning. Wayne's car led the way, the pickup following close behind. Men erupted from the vehicles, their voices competing with Red's vocal efforts.

A minute later, Brand was bundling Dena into the pickup. Nick sat behind the wheel and Red had been sternly told to remain in the bed of the truck. Wayne stood off to one side with Jay. Dena examined his impassive expression and turned to Brand as he closed her door. Resting her hand on his, she waited until his gray eyes met hers. "He's worth saving," she said quietly.

Brand dropped his hand is if it had been stung and stepped back. "I can't make any promises," he said grimly. "Take her back to the house, Nick." His eyes flicked back to hers. "Will you wait for me? I'll be there as soon as I can."

Two hours later, Dena prowled from one room to another. She was bathed, powdered, dressed and restless. Where on earth was Brand? She turned her thoughts away from racks and thumbscrews. They aren't used anymore, she reminded herself. Especially by people like Brand and Jay. They're good men, she thought for the hundredth time. They'll resolve the whole thing in a civilized manner. But she'd feel a lot better, she admitted, if she had something more concrete than instinct to base that opinion on.

Her heart jumped at the sound of the doorbell, then settled back in place. Brand would have used his key. Hurrying into the hallway, she called to Nick, "I'll get it."

At least one good thing had come out of this. Nick was talking to her. He'd mumbled a couple of comments in the truck and apparently realized that it wasn't all that difficult. Since then, he had talked nonstop. She smiled as she reached the door. He had also given her the recipe for the muffins and agreed to go up in the balloon.

Tom Norris stood grinning down at her. "You've had yourself a busy day, haven't you?"

She nodded agreeably and opened the door wider. "Come in and tell me what you've been up to."

"Can't. I have to get back to the office." He held up her purse. "You left this in Randall's car. Brand asked me to drop it by and to give you this." He placed an envelope on top of her clutch bag and handed them both to her.

Chuckling at her frustrated expression, he said, "Cheer up. Brand should be along soon. He'll tell you what's been going on. In the meantime, keep out of trouble." With that, he waved and loped back to his car.

Keep out of trouble. Funny man. She glared at the car until it was out of sight. Retracing her steps, she tossed the bag on the sofa and dropped down beside it. She frowned at the envelope. Another typewritten message was the last thing in the world she needed—or wanted. What in heaven's name was keeping him so long?

Moodily she slipped a finger in the flap of the envelope and tore it across. The loosely creased sheet of paper dropped in her lap and unfolded.

Dena,
    We're working things out, but it's taking longer than I expected. Wait for me. Please.
                                        Brand

Dena stared in disbelief. It was terse. To the point, no frills. Typical of Brand. But, most important of all, it was *written*. He could have asked Tom to tell her he'd be late, but he had chosen to write. She knew, as with everything else he did, that it had been a deliberate decision.

But had he really considered all of the ramifications of his action? she wondered. Whether he realized it or not, he had sent her two messages—one, briefly informative; the other, an admission of trust. From the very beginning, despite his skepticism, he had bluntly informed her that he wanted and intended to have her. Was it remotely possible, even probable, that he was telling her his doubt had turned to trust, wanting to loving? That he loved her enough to risk revealing himself?

Grinning idiotically, Dena stretched out on the couch, holding the paper above her. Actually, there wasn't a heck of a lot that she hadn't already figured out. He had a high energy level and fantastic work capacity. He was objective, aggressive, highly sensual, and would probably be hell to live with.

Her eyebrows raised as she considered the upper zones of his letters. Idealistic. He was also extremely sincere and loyal. One might even say that he had a noble character, for whether he was right or wrong in judgment, he would always act in accordance with his principles. Sitting up, she took one last satisfied look at the writing. She could leave Wayne safely in Brand's hands.

"Hey, Dena," Nick called. "Want to help me bake some bread?"

Considering the decibel level in the kitchen, she thought, Nick must be using every available utensil and pan. She might as well help. Dena folded the note and stuffed it in her purse. An amused, very feminine smile curved her lips. She could see that Brand's love letters were going to be as original as the man himself.

"Hi."

Dena lazily opened her eyes at the sound of Brand's deep voice. The first thing she saw was her bare toes. They were pressed against the edge of the hot tub, just above the line of frothy water. She tilted her head, raising her gaze a notch, and decided that the scenery had undergone a definite improvement. Brand stood before her in a brief, sleek, navy-blue bathing suit. He was a man who wore clothes well and who wore next to nothing even better.

Her eyes skimmed up long, muscular legs and thighs to the stretchy material that barely covered what society dictated should be concealed in polite company. Her gaze reluctantly left the narrow hips and moved up to a stomach, rib cage and chest adorned with slabs of muscle and an inverted arrow of dark hair. Her eyes widened in appreciation at a wedge of shoulders before lifting to his face. A face that had once seemed so cold and hard and was now so...necessary.

He made no move to join her; he was examining her with interest, obviously approving of what golden flesh wasn't concealed by a combination of foam and bikini.

He grinned. "We ought to do this more often."

"Get in a hot tub?" she inquired blandly.

"Not exactly." He stepped forward and eased down beside her. "Do you realize this is the first time I've seen you when you haven't been wrapped in material from head to toe?"

"Shocking," she murmured, scooting over to make room for him. He draped his arm around her shoulders, drawing her against him. They leaned back and let the warm water flow over them, looking up at the canopy of stars glimmering in the dark sky. "Nice," she sighed.

He turned, lifting her as if she weighed no more than a handful of foam and deposited her in his lap. His arms held her close as he leaned back again. "Nice," he agreed. "Did you get my message?" he asked, breaking the comfortable silence.

Message, not note. The man was getting downright subtle. She nodded. "I got it." Before he could comment, she looked up expectantly. "Tell me what happened. All of it. Every word."

"He's going to get help," he told her. "That's the bottom line."

She struggled to sit up and was hauled back against his chest.

"You might have noticed," she pointed out politely, "that I asked for all the lines, not just the bottom."

He groaned, closed his eyes and fitted her more precisely against his body. "Dena, you feel so damn good in my arms, I can hardly think, much less work my way through all the complications we've handled today."

She turned and eased her arms around his neck. The softness of her breasts pressed against his chest and he groaned again. Smiling, she kissed his chin.

"You're right. It does feel good. If you'd hurry and tell me what happened," she tempted, "we could concentrate on exactly how good it is."

His eyelids lifted and silvery eyes gleamed with interest. "Promise?"

She nodded.

"Wayne told us the same thing he told you, only more in detail. It was burnout." He sighed sharply. "Fatigue and depression are a hell of a combination to fight." Dena listened to him talk, absently running a finger down the dark mat of hair on his chest. His hand caught hers as it neared his waist and moved it back to his neck. "If you want me to make any sense at all, you'd better keep your hands right where they are," he commented.

"Burnout," she prompted.

"So we're packing him off for a vacation that includes counseling," he repeated, cutting it short. "When he's ready, he'll be back."

"With a clean slate?"

"Yes. No one will know why he's gone."

"Everyone in Security already knows about it," she pointed out.

A faint lift at the corner of his mouth reassured her. "False alarm," he said laconically. "By now, they all know that your jaunt this morning had nothing to do with the leak."

"Oh? Exactly what were we doing?" she asked with interest.

"Having a private conversation," he said vaguely. "A long one." She made a face of disappointment. Stung, he said, "I couldn't think of anything else. I just said it in a tone of authority and no one questioned me."

She didn't doubt that. "Jay's people will still be looking for someone," she reminded him. "How are you going to call off the hounds?"

The other corner of his mouth lifted. "That's another nice thing about being the boss," he said lazily. "I don't have to give anyone an explanation. Tomorrow Jay will announce to his staff that the case is closed. Because of certain confidential information, there is to be no further discussion. Period."

She laced her hands in his hair and tugged. When his head lowered, she kissed him softly on the lips. "You're a good man, Brand McAllister." Even in the dim light she could see a flush burn his cheeks.

He shrugged his massive shoulders. "We send alcoholics and drug addicts for treatment. Why shouldn't we take care of someone whose only mistake was working too hard?"

She grinned at his belligerent tone. "No reason at all." Changing the subject abruptly, she asked, "Will you let me check his writing before he goes back to work?"

"Of course."

Dena brought her arms down and wedged her elbows against his chest, eyeing him with suspicion. "Why are you so agreeable all of a sudden?"

"Because I have an open mind."

"Hah!"

"And," he continued as if she hadn't spoken, "because I'm a practical man. You and your profession are a package deal. If I want one, I damn well better understand the other." He drew her back against him. "Now," he asked abruptly, "are you through torturing me?"

"One more question."

He groaned.

"Did Wayne do any irreparable damage with the information he leaked?"

"No. And that saved him. We hadn't reached the critical stage when he flipped. If we had, or if we hadn't quit work on the project until we found out who was doing it, I don't know what would have happened to him. We're all lucky it turned out this way."

He felt the last residue of tension leave her body. "Satisfied?" he asked in a low voice.

"Um-hmm."

"Dena—" his voice was urgent, all humor gone "—now—"

"Hey, boss," Nick shouted from the kitchen window, "did you have any dinner?"

Brand's oaths were voluble and nasty. "No," he said violently.

"God, you must be starved. No wonder you're yelling. I'll get something out there right away."

Before Brand could protest, Nick flipped on the porch light and opened the kitchen door. Dena snickered at Brand's savage expression and slid off his lap.

"We baked some bread today," Nick told him, "and I just made some sandwiches." He plunked a tray beside Brand's elbow. "Is this enough?" he asked, dropping down into a patio chair.

While Brand was scowling at the plate and the man who brought it, Dena asked, "If you're not going to eat them all, may I have one? I didn't eat much at dinner." Reaching for a thick meat sandwich, she winked at Nick. He had watched in admiration as she'd packed away a meal that would have done credit to a lumberjack. But Brand needed food. He wouldn't deny her, and if she was occupied he might as well join her.

Brand ate quickly and with total concentration. He even drank the glass of milk. He choked once, when Nick told Dena, "You have to keep him fed. He has a hell of a temper when he's hungry."

Brand set the glass down and made sure Dena was finished. His level gaze lifted Nick from the chair. "Thank you," he said with commendable calm. "Now go away while I propose to Dena." A grinning Nick picked up the tray and thumped his way across the deck. The kitchen door slammed and the light went off.

Dena blinked, as much from shock as to adjust her eyes to the sudden darkness. Brand didn't have any trouble, she noted. He simply reached out and gathered her into his arms. She went willingly, but her brows drew together in a frown. Just like that, she wondered. Go away while I propose? Didn't the man have a shred of romance in his soul?

"Dena, I—"

The peal of the telephone was startling in the darkness.

Brand muttered something under his breath that she was just as glad she didn't understand.

"Aren't you going to answer it?" she asked, as it rang again.

"Nick will get it." His voice was taut. "Dena—"

"Boss—" Nick's voice floated out the window "—it's Charlie. He says he has to talk to you."

"I don't believe it," Brand muttered. He raised his voice. "Tell him—"

Dena hugged him around the waist, then released him. "Answer it," she urged. "It might be important."

Brand's lips touched her eyebrow and slid to her temple before he sighed and reached for the phone. "Charlie? This better be good."

Dena curled up next to him, smiling at his truculent tone.

"Do I know anything about *what*? Jute? It's growing wild on the island and you want to help the natives start a business?" he repeated in a stunned voice. "Wait a minute." He looked down at Dena. "Do you know what jute is used for?"

She couldn't control the laughter that welled up at his distracted expression. "Rope," she gurgled. "Burlap and gunny sacks." Quivering, she listened as he relayed the information.

"Damn it, Charlie, I don't care if the stuff is falling out of trees like bananas instead of growing in neat little rows. And if they're still shooting arrows at visitors, I don't imagine the natives care either." He listened in growing impatience before saying, "No, I do not want to order any burlap bags. I don't *care* if they need motivation. They're your project, you encourage them."

He held the receiver so Dena could listen to Charlie plaintively ask what he would do with a load of gunny sacks.

"Charlie—" Brand's quiet voice was full of menace "—for all I care, you can—"

Dena reached out and pressed a button, cutting off the conversation. She took the receiver and placed it on the deck.

Brand scowled at her. "Where were we?" he demanded.

Dena's eyes sparkled with laughter. "I think the next item on the agenda was a proposal."

"Ah." He looked down at the turbulent water. "How do you feel about it?"

"About what?" she asked, carefully blank. There was a limit, she decided. It was one thing to save a casual note and call it a love letter, but she wasn't going to settle for a nonexistent proposal.

"About my question," he said in a tight voice.

"I haven't heard one."

He glared at her, looking anything but loverlike. "Damn it, Dena, I want to know if you'll marry me, and you know it."

Her steady gaze challenged him. "Tell me why," she demanded softly.

Brand's movements were slow, but there was nothing uncertain about them. He turned to face her. Leaning over, he rested his hands on the frame of the tub, enclosing her between his arms. Her eyes widened and he saw the uncertainty in them. She needed to hear the words, he realized. She deserved them. If he hoped to have this warm and loving woman in his arms, his home, and his bed, he'd better say them.

"Dena, my maddening love," he said in a ragged voice, "I want you to be a part of me, a part of my life. I need you in ways I never dreamed of, to share laughter, to remind me to admire the leaves before I decide how far back to cut the branches, and to make me whole."

His silvery gaze took in her vulnerable expression and he ached to kiss her. "But most of all," he continued, "I want you here so I can love you. You touch something inside of me, arouse me as no other woman has or ever will. I need you so much I ache from head to toe, but for the first time in my life, I'm afraid to reach out and take what I want. You have to be willing to come to me, to—"

Dena pressed a shaking finger over his lips, tears sliding down her cheeks. "Enough, my love," she whispered. "I'll marry you, gladly."

"Why?" he demanded gently, his need to know as great as hers.

She sniffed. "Would you believe that I work for this foundation that's doing a study on left-brained people and I need you for research?" she asked weakly. A tremor shook her body. Brand smiled and shifted her to his lap.

"No," he said. "Should I?"

She shook her head. "No. I'll marry you because you're what I've been looking for all of my life, my other half. I want to watch your face light up when I walk into a room. I want to wake up each morning in your arms. I want—"

Her words were halted by the urgent touch of his lips.

"Brand," she murmured, "tomorrow when I wake up, I want to be in your arms." His lips came to a halt in the sweet curve of her neck.

His silvery eyes glittered as they surveyed her. "I want you for a lifetime," he told her flatly, "not just one night. You'll wake up that way the morning after you become Mrs. Brand McAllister."

Her head rested comfortably against his shoulder. "You own an airplane, don't you?" she asked thoughtfully.

He nodded. "The firm does."

"Could it take us to Las Vegas or Reno?"

"When?"

"Tonight."

He exhaled softly, never taking his eyes from her face. "Yes."

Her smile was as old as Eve, as full of promise as a rainbow. "Then what are we waiting for?"

COMING NEXT MONTH

AFTER THE MUSIC—Diana Palmer
Rock singer Sabina Cane had been warned that Hamilton Thorndon
was a formidable man, but nothing could have prepared her for the
impact he would have on her life.

FAMILY SECRETS—Ruth Langan
Who was blackmailing Trudy St. Martin? Caine St. Martin and
Ivy Murdock joined forces to discover the culprit's identity, and in
the process they discovered the secrets of love.

THE HIGHEST TOWER—Ann Hurley
BeeGee was fearless enough to join the Greenings in their work as
steeplejacks, but when her heart started falling for Dan Greening
she became determined to keep her feet firmly on the ground.

HEART SHIFT—Glenda Sands
Arson…someone had burned down Chris's shop. Chris felt lucky
that handsome and imposing Ian West was on the case, until he told
her that she was the prime suspect.

THE CATNIP MAN—Barbara Turner
Julia treated life as a serious matter until, aboard a Mississippi
riverboat, she met Chad. His infectious good nature chipped away
at her reserve and brought laughter and love to her heart.

MINE BY WRITE—Marie Nicole
Professor Kyle McDaniels gladly offered to help Mindy Callaghan
with her writing, yet when it came to offering his heart, he was the
one who needed a little help.

AVAILABLE NOW:

WRITTEN ON THE WIND
Rita Rainville

GILDING THE LILY
Emilie Richards

KINDRED HEARTS
Lacey Springer

EYE OF THE BEHOLDER
Charlotte Nichols

NOW OR NEVER
Arlene James

CHRISTMAS MASQUERADE
Debbie Macomber